SPECIES

EDITED BY
SIGNIFICANTOTTER

A THURSTON HOWL PUBLICATIONS BOOK

SPECIES: OTTERS

Edited by SignificantOtter
Cover art by Kippy © 2019

A Thurston Howl Publications Book
Published by Thurston Howl Publications
thurstonhowlpublications.com
Lansing, MI

CONTENTS

SONNET: TO THE RIVER OTTER
Samuel Taylor Coleridge

Dear native brook! wild streamlet of the West!
How many various-fated years have passed,
What happy and what mournful hours, since last
I skimmed the smooth thin stone along thy breast,
Numbering its light leaps! Yet so deep impressed
Sink the sweet scenes of childhood, that mine eyes
I never shut amid the sunny ray,
But straight with all their tints thy waters rise,
Thy crossing plank, thy marge with willows grey,
And bedded sand that, veined with various dyes,
Gleamed through thy bright transparence! On my way,
Visions of childhood! oft have ye beguiled
Lone manhood's cares, yet waking fondest sighs:
Ah! that once more I were a careless child!

OTTER HAIKU
Translated by SignificantOtter

獺の
祭見て来よ
瀬田の奥
芭蕉

I came here to see
otters fish at the river
deep in Seta's hills
—Matsuo Bashō

茶器どもを
獺の祭の
並べ方
正岡子規

I prepare my tea
like the otter offers fish
so neatly arranged
—Masaoka Shiki

The term containing otter in these poems (獺祭, or dassai) is translated literally as 'otter festival.' This phrase is frequently used as symbolism in Japanese poetry. Japanese otters, before their extinction, had the habit of catching fish and lining them up on the riverbank or in their nest before eating them. Many Japanese festivals involve the placing of religious offerings, so this similar-appearing otter behavior led to the term 'otter festival.'

However, 'dassai' has evolved into both a poetic marker of spring and an idiom for a person who collects books on their desk before diving into them to study. The famous haiku author Masaoka Shiki used this word "Dassai" as his pen name. His most famous poetry is collected in the volume "Talks on Haiku from the Otter's Den."

Jessica Paddock

Jessica Paddock splits her time between thinking about writing and actually doing it. She likes to explore mythology, pretend she knows how to swim so to not upset the otters, eat way too many jellybeans, and lurk in the shadows of Washington forests. You can chat with her on Twitter @Imagining_Ink.

DANCE WITH THE DEVIL

When Sylvie was five, her grandfather locked away her visions in a plastic bottle.

It had to be done. For a while her visions had been harmless—minor dreams of the future, shapes in the mirror no one else could see—but then she almost drowned chasing a vision to the bottom of the lake. She had been so scared she couldn't swim for a year. So her parents let Grandpappy seal them away. It was a choice between that and leaving the lake—and for an otter family, that was no choice at all.

So she lived without visions. She grew up, moved out, went to beauty school. It was easy—often she forgot they had ever existed. But sometimes she would stare into the city pool and wonder what it would be like to see something staring back. She would wonder if a part of her was missing.

And then, twenty years after she almost drowned, she looked into the salon mirror as she trimmed a tiger's cheek fur and saw something looking back. It was just a glimpse—just a flicker of a silhouette, a suggestion of yellow eyes, a jagged curve of horns—and then it was gone. She stood frozen, scissors gripped like a weapon, searching the vast mirror for anything out of the ordinary, until at last the tiger said, "Miss?"

It had only been a glimpse, but that was enough. It was hard to focus when she kept scanning the mirrors for anything dark and unfriendly, and she only forced herself to stop rushing through her work when she almost chopped a client's ear off. She even rushed through closing, cleaning as her two coworkers got ready to leave so they could all go together.

Was her magic outgrowing its bonds? Not many people

knew about this kind of stuff, so it was hard to get answers without going to a specialist.

That night she lay in bed, staring up at the ceiling. Her boyfriend's arms were wrapped around her almost painfully tight, a line of his drool seeping into her neck fur, every inch of him the epitome of snuggly Golden Retriever.

"Do you think I should talk to Grandpappy?" she asked.

Kevin grumbled at the broken quiet. "I'm telling you, the chemicals of that place are making you see things. And isn't he, like, a hermit now or something?"

"What about a specialist?"

"Those quacks? You don't need anyone to tell you what you what to do."

He was right, of course. She didn't need help. She was too strong to go running to someone else the moment anything went wrong. Still, that morning she managed to extract herself from him with minimal fur loss and go to the city pool early. She stared into the surface, but there was nothing. No vision, no figure. Just a ratty little otter looking back.

That week at work, she kept getting glimpses of something in the mirror. A flicker of a shadow when she moved her head, gone the moment she focused. Eyes with horizontal slits peering out from beneath the clawwork table behind her station. Mostly she had the feeling of being watched. It was a crawling spider up her spine, a chill that slowly crept along her fur like a glacier overtaking the land, carving out valleys in her nerves.

And so here she was, working at a snail's pace to keep her paranoia from messing her up, feeling like a pup as something that might not even exist stared her down.

Ridiculous.

A week after she almost skewered herself on a hedgehog's spines, Sylvie took her time to close. Her coworkers left, and she was alone in a room of mirrors and chairs with nothing but a mop gripped tight in her paws. With the music gone and the lights dimmed, the place was eerily quiet, the distant hum of cars making her feel as if she was the only person in the world, as if she could just turn out the lights and disappear as well. A car passed on the road outside, throwing her shadow from one side of the room to the other.

"Enough is enough," she said through gritted teeth. She dug her claws into the wood of the mop. "Come out and face me, or leave forever. I don't have time to deal with this."

Nothing happened.

She bared her teeth. "You're going to get me fired! Do you have any idea what this job means to me? It's the only thing I'm good at!"

Still nothing. No eyes with horizontal slits, no shape in the mirror—just a rumpled otter with a broom in her paws, looking small and alone in the vast reflection of the salon.

At last she said, voice quiet, "Do you... do you want to talk? Are you just—?"

She growled and shoved her mop into the bucket, face burning as she scrubbed at the floor. "Stupid. This is all stupid. Talking to nothing in an empty room! Ugh, Kevin was right. I'm just—"

She froze. There was something next to her in the mirror, a shadow with jagged horns and yellow eyes, so tall it had to hunch to not scrape against the top of the frame. They stood for a moment, a perfect picture of hunter and prey. Then the shadow shifted, reaching slowly towards her within the reflection, a clawed finger hovering above her trembling shoulder.

A car swept by, throwing their shadows across the mirrors, a kaleidoscope of horn and claw and a frozen rictus of terror reflecting back again and again into some esoteric painting, and then the thing was gone.

She stood frozen in the salon, alone.

If anything, Sylvie's little "chat" only made things worse. Now the thing appeared outside of work as well.

And it was braver than ever. Not only did it flicker in her bathroom mirror and peer out from the surface of drinking glasses, its shape growing more distinct each day, but sometimes she would feel a cold claw trailing lines down her spine or see the rocking chair in her bedroom creak slowly back and forth. Her dreams swarmed with shadows, and often she woke to a smell of sulfur she could not scrub from her fur, no matter how hard she dug. She had taken to covering mirrors when she changed.

She was being haunted. Maybe it was a ghost, maybe it was something else—but it was haunting her, and she wasn't sure what to do about it.

"You're imagining things," Kevin would tell her each time, until she finally gave up mentioning it at all.

But the pressure to say something built. Almost a month after it all started, she sat down for Saturday game night with her friends and found herself regaling them with stories of her new hang-on.

"Sounds like a demon," said Diane, a shrew who tended to know such things. Kevin frowned at his cards, but he didn't interrupt as she went on. "My uncle got haunted by one once. He said it chewed on one of his toes, and his toe got infected and they had to cut it off."

"Nonsense," Kevin growled. "Are we playing this game or not? Di, it's your turn."

"How did he get rid of it?" Sylvie asked.

"Oh, he didn't. It followed him to the war, and he died."

Sylvie shivered. Almost a dozen of them were crammed around the table. These people knew Kevin much better than they knew her, but there was safety in numbers, so she didn't mind talking about it. The thing—the demon?—hadn't done anything to hurt her so far, but the unknown held a certain danger. But here, sitting with her friends, it felt more like a story than something real.

She smiled at Kevin, but he was still scowling at his cards. She nudged him playfully, which she realized was a mistake when he swiveled to her, got abruptly to his feet, and said, "Let's go get another drink."

Her beer was still half full, but she knew that tone. She politely excused them and following him up the stairs, watching his rigid scruff twitch with every step. When they got to the kitchen, she opened her mouth, but he spun around and grabbed her arms.

"Enough with the ghost shit," he snarled, voice quiet but tense.

She was so rattled she could only think to say, "I never said it was a ghost."

His expression darkened further, ears so flat against his skull they seemed to disappear. She could count each one of his bone-white teeth, and in an instant of heat-of-the-moment clarity, she noted how well he cared for them.

"Just knock it off, okay? They're going to think you're a freak or you're making it up for attention. I don't want them to think there's something wrong with you—or me."

She wished she could jump into the sink and follow the pipes into the river, where she wouldn't have to worry about a demon or her reputation or how much his claws hurt.

She gently pushed a hand against his arm. "Let go, Kev."

He squeezed her one more time and then let go. His face twisted into a guilty expression. "I'm sorry, honey. But you know I'm just looking out for you, right?"

"No, you're right. I wasn't thinking."

He pulled her into a hug, and though it was the last thing she wanted right now, she forced herself not to push away.

He ran his fingers through the fur on the back of her neck.

"I just want us to be normal. Okay?"

She pushed her nose into his chest, breathing his strawberry shampoo. "Okay."

Sylvie's arms still stung the next morning as she shuffled into the bathroom. She was so sleepy that it took her moment to notice the message scrawled on the mirror with red lipstick: *HE'S A DICK.*

She clapped her paws over her mouth to smother a panicked giggle, her mind spinning.

"What is it?" Kevin mumbled from the other room, still in bed.

Sylvie hastily shut the door. "Nothing!"

She pumped soap onto a wet cloth and started to clean the mirror, then stopped and took a picture. This, at least, was something she hadn't imagined. Kevin couldn't fight fact. Yet her finger hovered over the "send" button. Would this just make things worse?

She shoved her phone into her pocket and picked up the cloth. "You're the dick," she said, scrubbing the mirror. "That was my favorite shade."

She heard a distant rustle of dry leaves and wondered if the demon was laughing.

That night Kevin took her out for dinner, the sort of wordless apology Sylvie gladly accepted when it included seafood paella. She caught glimpses of the demon in her wine glass, but she stayed silent. Kevin was in a good mood. No need to ruin that with her personal freakshow.

And personal it was. No one else seemed to notice the demon, who grew increasingly bolder as the weeks went on. It was no longer content to flicker at the edge of her vision. Now she would see it in the mirror as she worked, a hunched, mirage-like figure watching her trim fur and style whiskers. She couldn't make out its details. It was as if the thing was standing deep in the shadows of an evening forest, and though she occasionally caught glimpses of ragged fur or the black gloss of its horns, it seemed content to stay between the trees. Except for its eyes—yellow with horizontal slit pupils, like an exaggerated version of a goat's. No matter how faded the creature was, those eyes were always visible. So visible, in fact, they seemed to glow like a cat's in the dark.

But no one else said anything. She was on her own.

The message in the mirror haunted her. She wanted to send the picture to some kind of supernatural forum and see if anyone else could tell her what its implications were, but something stopped her. A few days later at work, looking at the shadow in the mirror as she trimmed a highland cow's fur out of his eyes, she realized what it was. The demon would know if she talked to someone else about this. And it was not fear of retaliation that stopped her. She just didn't want to be rude.

That night she was slow to close, leaving herself alone in the salon again. She reinstated a tradition she had abandoned almost two months ago, plugging her phone into the speakers and letting classical music spill into the air. The demon watched from a chair in the mirror as she hummed and cleaned and spun about the room. A few times, she thought she heard another voice joining in.

Sylvie made a choice. She was done sitting around and letting this thing haunt her, occasionally being almost friendly and then acting like nothing had happened.

"Which one?" she asked the bathroom mirror, holding up two shirts. If they were going to live together, then she might as well make an effort to accept the olive branch the demon may or may not be aware it was extending.

For a long moment nothing happened. Her heart pounded as she wondered if the mirror would just shatter, or if the sink would hiss to life and soak her, or if the demon would just refuse to acknowledge her ridiculous question and leave her standing here for the rest of the night looking like an idiot. But then, finally, a shadow slowly rose from behind her until it practically filled the mirror. They stood in silence, an otter and a demon facing off.

It pointed to the green shirt.

She tried not to sigh in relief as she held it against herself. "Good choice. Green looks great with my fur." She added a soft white hat and a black jacket and faced the mirror, hands on her hips. "Well? How do I look?"

The shadow stared at her with unblinking eyes, pupils slowly contracting into almost nothing. Then it flickered and disappeared.

Kevin cracked open the door. "Who are you talking to?"

"Your sense of privacy. Which is to say, nothing. Ready to go?"

They headed to the club. Kevin was shit at dancing, but sometimes he deigned to join her for classical night, which he could manage without looking, in his eyes, like a total fool. Mostly, though, he liked to watch her like a hawk, steering her away from any men who wanted to join her, even the ones there to dance, not flirt. Sometimes she felt like a piece of territory. But still, he tried.

That night, as she taught him the steps to the tango, her phone buzzed. She took it in the bathroom.

"I'm sorry," her father said. "We found him just last night. It looked like he'd been there for a while, but we didn't—well, you know how he is. Was."

Grandpappy was dead. She tried to wrap her mind around the concept, but it was like trying to touch a reflection on the water.

"We're going to clean out his cabin this weekend. Would you...?"

"I'll come."

Sylvie barely saw the demon following her as she numbly collected Kevin from the dance floor. She told him in the car, though there wasn't much to tell—her grandfather died in his cabin, and it had taken weeks for anyone to notice. That was hardly a shock. Sylvie had always known he would die like that, alone and rotting like the hermit he had become after his wife died.

She wasn't sure how to feel. They had never been close, even when she was young. She would always find him watching her, as if waiting for her to snap and do something dangerous. Sometimes he would shove burning sticks of strange smells under her nose and ask if she felt anything. To him, she would always be nothing more than a child full of visions.

And a part of her thought she would never forgive him for taking those away.

Despite all that, it hurt. He was dead. She should be sad, but there was no reason to want to curl up into herself and wail until her lungs burst. There was no reason for this broken bird keening in her chest. She was strong. She should not be shattered by the death of someone she had not talked to in years.

"Do you have to go?" Kevin asked the next day as she packed. "The rest of your family lives way closer. Can't they take care of it?"

Her spare belt jumped as she reached for it. She frowned and looked to Kevin, but his back was turned. "I want to do this."

"No, you don't. Your dad just tricked you into it so they wouldn't have to do all the work."

"Kev, Grandpappy's dead!"

"He was a jerk. You didn't like him, and he didn't like you. Who cares?"

She twisted the belt in her hands, feeling the edges bite into her skin. He was right, of course. This should not be so hard. But couldn't he see that it hurt anyway?

"Hey, come on. Don't get mad at me." He was suddenly behind her, pressing his palms against her shoulder blades. His breath tickled her ear. "You know I love you."

She leaned back into him. "Then will you go with me?"

His weight disappeared. "What? No. You know they don't like me."

"They don't—" She closed her eyes, taking a deep breath. Now was not the time for this old argument. "Just come with me, okay? You can finally see the lake."

"No way. Your family would probably drown me or something."

She squeezed her eyes shut. Her head hurt too much for this. Eventually she found the strength to say, "I'm going," and that was the end of that.

She left Saturday morning. Kevin watched her go, an unspoken tension in the air. The demon kept appearing in her rearview mirrors, almost making her swerve off the road more than once. It was annoying, but least *someone* came with her.

She had hoped to catch sight of the lake after the three hour drive to Grandpappy's house, but overgrown trees covered the view. A few people had come: her parents, her brother, some cousins. They had left the attic alone. They seemed to know that finding the bottle was something she had to do herself. But she felt embarrassed somehow, so she left it for later.

They worked throughout the day. It was hard, sweaty work—Grandpappy had been a bit of a hoarder, and thanks to all the strange and sometimes supernatural things he kept, they had to be careful moving stuff around. Sylvie kept expecting a cool breeze to blow off the lake and bring her back to childhood, back to swimming with her brothers and fishing with her mother, back to building dinky boats with her schoolmates, full of energy and fearing nothing. But it didn't, and so she just did her best to avoid looking at the empty patch of flooring in the living room, where there had once been a carpet and Grandpappy's favorite chair.

She called Kevin as her family locked up the moving van for the night. He listened to her talk for a few minutes, then said he was at game night and had to go. He hung up before she could reply.

"You sure you want to stay in this place alone?" asked one of her cousins, the most supernaturally minded of the group. "Having someone here will help keep things steady, but it might be spooky."

"I'll be fine."

She watched them drive away, disappearing into the trees and leaving her alone with an empty house that had for so long held a dead man.

Much of her family lived on the other side of the lake, just off the water. They fished. They swam. They stayed. She could have gone with them, slept on the couch of her childhood home, maybe swam in the lake with her family in the morning, just as she had done every day until she left it all behind. Instead, she went back into the cabin.

Grandpappy had sealed her visions away in a plastic soda bottle. She couldn't remember it very well, since he had never let her into the attic to see it, but she figured she would recognize it anyway. The attic was dusty and crammed with boxes and old furniture and all the odds and ends one would expect from a long life ended abruptly. She thought she might have trouble finding the bottle, but it was waiting for her, sitting on a rickety old desk with its label torn away and its cap more brown than white. It was cracked, and it was empty.

She looked back, where the demon was watching her through a dusty mirror.

"Is this why everything's happening?" she asked. "Is this why you're here?"

The demon bowed its head. Then it was gone.

They finished packing the next day. She took half a box of things—nothing important or even magical, but her parents had insisted she lighten their load. The empty soda bottle sat on the hood of her car. She was not sure who had put it there or what she should do with it. What good was an empty bottle?

She decided to stay the night again, not sure she could handle being around anyone else. It was too early to sleep and they had already eaten, so there was not much to do except head down to the lake.

Sometimes she missed the lake, an ache too deep for city pools to heal. She would wake up in the middle of the night with the taste of fresh water on her tongue and remember the feeling of depth all around her, of a lake-bottom blooming murk and bugs and fish beneath her touch. Sometimes she would feel so nostalgic she wanted to puke. Kevin dismissed it as crazy otter stuff. A few times he got so annoyed that he plucked the fur on her arms, demanding to know which was more real—the pain or her memories.

He couldn't understand. She lay on her back in the lake, feeling the water against her fur. It felt heavier than pool water, more meaningful, as if it held its own ancient history in every drop, as if the lake could remember everything that ever drank from it or touched its surface, imprinted with hundreds or thousands of years of existing.

If he couldn't understand this, could he understand her?

She closed her eyes. The dipping sun painted her eyelids red. She could feel her own heartbeat in the water, its pace going faster and faster as she squeezed the fur on her stomach, fighting against her quickening pulse. Could anyone understand? Her family had been somber and respectful as they packed up Grandpappy's life, and she felt sad too—of course she felt sad—but could they ever understand that she wanted to take that plastic bottle and burn it? Would they even understand that part of the reason she was upset was that she would never be allowed to scream at him? Would they understand her regret—not that she had spent so little time with him, but that she had not been angry enough?

She pressed her paws to her eyes. She was shaking. She was alone in the lake and she knew now that it was a deeper alone, not just a physical space but a family she hardly spoke to and a boyfriend who plucked fur from her arms and did not care that someone was dead. A boyfriend who danced with her when it suited him and stopped swimming a few months after they moved in together, wrinkling his nose at the smell of chlorine. A boyfriend who was not here, and a family on the other side of a lake that suddenly seemed as vast as an ocean. A grandfather who was dead. An empty bottle. A heart too weak to take it.

A keening rose within her. The broken bird squirmed up through her chest and into her throat, hollow bones pricking holes in her flesh, its rot infesting her like pollution infesting the lake she had left behind. She wanted to cry. She wanted to scream into the water and let air bubble up around her. She wanted to disappear into the lake, to become part of its history instead of an otter so pathetic she had almost drowned. Instead of the remnants of a girl so spooked by a vision she had refused to swim for a year.

An *otter* who had refused to swim. She tried so hard to distance herself from that girl, to be stronger than some sniveling pup, but she was still just a paper boat on the lake battered aside by the slightest of breezes.

She sank. Water encased her, slipping around her whiskers as she sought its comfort, but all she could remember was the light deep within the murk, further than a little girl should ever go. She remembered the call—a sweet singing without words, a gentle brush of fingers against her cheek. The singing filled her now, shoving away the broken bird with its broken calls, lightening the great weight of her thoughts until she was free. Her tears dissolved in the water. She had forgotten how beautiful the lake was when the sun no longer touched it.

The light sang her deeper. She wanted to sing too, to release the useless air from her lungs, to fill herself with water and go deeper and deeper until the sun could never burn her again. She could be happy if she reached the bottom. No more dead family, no more empty bottles, no more boyfriends who could never understand. No more pretending she was strong.

The vision sang, her heart lightened, and she reached for the bottom.

A shadow flickered across the light. She jerked back, heart skipping a beat, and in that moment the illusion shattered. Her lungs burned, her body ached, and the dark murk of the lake swirled around her. She felt as if she had just stepped away from a crowded concert, the sudden stillness feeling alien and haunting as her mind still pumped with the music and excitement she had left behind. She spun, trying to find which way was up. Something clamped onto her tail, but she kicked herself free and darted away. Red sunlight filtered weakly from above. She chased it, feeling a cool brush against her whiskers—but this was a comforting touch, and she clung to it with her mind.

She burst onto the surface, gasping for breath. She was halfway across the lake. The sun was setting.

By the time she heaved herself onto land, she could barely think. Her limbs shook. She shivered, scattering water from the surface of her fur. The lake was still warmed by the daylight long gone, but she shook so bad she could barely grip the shore. Her chest heaved like on ocean wave, and she puked up lakewater and half-digested pizza. This time she did not bother to fight her tears, dragging herself away from the lake and curling up among the trees. Two yellow eyes watched her from the shadows. She reached for them, and something cold brushed across her knuckles.

She shivered and cried and keened beneath the trees, and during it all she remembered the day many years ago when Grandpappy grew tired of her refusal to swim and took her out to the middle of the lake in his boat, dumped her there, and forced her to swim back on her own. That had been the start of her recovery, but she had hated him for it. She still hated him now, knowing there had been other ways to help her, unable to shake the imprint of that terror, even as she tried to forget the weakling she had been.

A nightbird called a mournful tune, and the demon hummed.

Kevin was not home when she got back to the apartment the next day. She could not work up the courage to call him. She texted Tiana to make sure the salon would be fine without her for the day—there was no way she trusted herself with scissors around someone's ears right now—and took a shower. It felt good to get the lake off her fur, even if the sight of it trickling down the drain made her chest constrict with mourning.

When she stepped out of the shower, a message awaited her on the fogged-up mirror:

Avizokal.

She hesitated, then touched the space beneath it. "Is that your name?"

The shadow in the mirror nodded.

"You know, I feel kind of rude called you 'it' all the time."

The demon paused for only a moment before it wrote another word: *she.*

The mirror was cool beneath Sylvie's touch. She closed her eyes. "Well. I guess it's nice to meet you at last, Avizokal. I hope we can be friends."

A hum tingled at the edge of her hearing.

She put Grandpappy's full-length mirror in the bedroom. It wasn't much, and the dark wood clashed with the lighter hues of the room, but she didn't plan on letting Kevin talk her out of this. She touched her forehead to it, breathing in familiar air. She couldn't tell Kevin what happened. He would just call it crazy otter stuff. He would say she was letting stress get to her. Maybe he would pluck fur from her arm and demand to know what was real.

She realized that she didn't want to be here when he got home, so she went in for the tail end of work. A few hours of washing fur and organizing products, and she started to feel more like herself. Tiana and Ken offered to go out for pizza with her, and though the offer made her want to burst into tears again, she suggested they do it another time. Not tonight. Tonight she waved them out, switched off the OPEN sign, and plugged her phone into the speakers.

Classical music spun in the air. It was so normal. She gripped her broom and breathed deep, inhaling the scents of fur products and cleaners. It was not as homey as the lake, but at least this place had not tried to kill her.

She could still feel it—the weight of the lake pressing onto her chest. Her tail twitched, as if trying to thrust her to the surface, but she was stuck here. Stuck with her pounding heart and memories that felt more real than any pain. Stuck in this state of weakness, even with the familiar scents and the music that normally made her want to dance, but now she just wanted to run away and hide in the dark. She dug her claws into the broom. Too weak. She was too weak.

Something cold touched her shoulder. She looked into the mirror. Avizokal hunched beside her, eyes softer than any demon's ought to be. Sylvie took a deep breath. She held up her hand, palm up, watching in the mirror as Avizokal touched it with her own. Music flowed through the empty room.

They danced. It was hard to stay together, stuck on

separate sides of the mirror, but they went slow. Sylvie stepped her familiar steps, and Avizokal followed the best she could, humming to the music, just a shadow stepping in time to an otter with a lake on her chest.

The song changed, their pace increased, and drop by drop the weight lessened.

"You should be careful."

Sylvie paused from scraping her plate clean and glanced up at Diane, who had just followed her into the kitchen. The shrew dug into the fridge.

"Huh?"

"That demon still bugging you?"

Sylvie glanced around, but Kevin was in the living room with the others. "Oh. Yeah."

"Talked to my aunt. She told me all kinds of crazy stuff. Like a demon who followed some fox all across the world, whispering to her how she would die. Or a demon who tricked someone into summoning it and took over his body, killing his family. Creepy stuff."

Sylvie shivered. But after what happened in the lake, it was hard to imagine her own demon as the most dangerous thing she had dealt with. "I'll keep my eyes open. But, um, look. Have you ever heard of a friendly demon?"

Diane paused, beer bottle in hand. She looked at Sylvie. "It's getting to you."

"It's—what?"

"The demon. I know it's real. Don't care what Kevin says— he's an ass anyway. We dated in high school. Did you know that?"

Sylvie's head spun to keep up with the conversation. "Um. No."

"Dumped him. He hit me."

They were silent for a moment. Diane stared at her beer.

Out of the corner of her eye, Sylvie saw Avizokal watching gravely from the reflection in the sink, her great horns twisted by the bending metal.

Diane looked back up at her. "They'll get into your head, you know. Tell you all kinds of things. Make you trust them. Make you love them. You'll call to them with all you have, and they'll come. They will. And that'll be the end of you. Because you meant it. That's what they do to you—they make you think they care. And they make you think that matters more than anything."

The fur on her arms stung.

Diane popped open the bottle with her teeth and tossed her the cap. "Got it?"

Sylvie felt the edge of the metal. It had bent under the shrew's hard teeth—no bottle opener, just raw force and two strong rows. "Yeah, I think so."

"Good. Now let's get back—those damn guys always try to start without me."

Sylvie kept the bottle cap in her pocket. She kept feeling the edge, the bend. The strength she always hoped she could have. She stared in the bathroom mirror, searching her eyes for anything she could grab hold of, anything within her that could stand tall. At the edge of her vision, Avizokal shifted into focus, staring at her. Sylvie touched the mirror, and Avizokal reached out a claw to meet her.

"What the hell is this?"

Sylvie jumped. She peered into the bedroom, where Kevin stood in front of the dresser holding a cracked plastic bottle.

"That's mine," she said. "It's—"

"I know it's *yours*. Why is it here?"

She hesitated, but she found it surprisingly easy to say, "Grandpappy kept my visions in it."

He opened his mouth for an instant reply, and then he

seemed to realize what she had said. "Why the hell do you have it?"

"I—I don't know. It feels right." She went to him. "Here, I'll move it—"

He held it away. "Well, it's trash."

Before she could think of a reply, he pushed her aside and tossed it into the garbage can.

"Kev!" She tried to reach for it, but he grabbed her arm.

"Leave it. I don't want trash sitting around."

He said it as if the matter had been decided. She clenched her fists, the bottle cap digging into her palm. To her own surprise, anger flared in her chest and she bared her teeth. "It wasn't sitting around! And it's not trash! Now *let go*."

He seemed as shocked as she was. But instead of releasing her, he furrowed his brows. She felt like something had broken free within her, something that rattled and spun in her chest, as if the little rotting bird had burned to ashes in the lake and been reborn into something vicious, something that could look at the dog in front of her and, for the first time, really see him— teeth neurotically whitened, hands half-curled towards fists, wide eyes hard and full of something sharp and brittle.

She loved him, and maybe he loved her. But that was not enough.

She drew herself up as best she could, well aware that she barely reached his sternum. Her heart thundered so hard she could barely hear her own words. "Kevin, this isn't working."

He yanked her and she stumbled, free hand slamming into the dresser for balance. Behind him, shadows roiled within the mirror.

"It would work just fine if you stopped being so selfish!" he snapped. He pulled her close so she could see his gleaming white fangs and smell his minty breath. "Where are you going to go if you leave me, huh? Your friends are *my* friends. Your coworkers don't care about you. Your family are back at that stupid lake. I'm your life!"

She looked into his eyes. They were deep and dark and furious. He really believed it. Some part of her believed it too, the part that wanted to press her face into the warmth of his chest and let him tell her that she didn't need anyone else, that she was full and complete as long as they stayed together, two pillars standing tall in this hurricane of a world.

But the rest of her remembered the long drive to the lake and the empty seat beside her. The stinging of her arm. The sneer on his lips.

She shoved herself away. His claws left behind stinging lines that welled with blood. She felt as if the world was compressing in her chest, trying to suck in her veins and nerves and lungs.

"You're not my life." she said. "We're *done*, Kev. This hurting, apologizing, moving on—it's bad. All of this is bad. I—" She closed her eyes tight, trying to fight back the tears. "I didn't realize until Diane said something. Until I heard that you hurt someone else. I thought, *How could someone do that to another person?* Now I realize the someone else is me, too. That I'm the one who's hurt. Which means you're the asshole who—"

A fist cracked against her face. She collapsed against the dresser, dazed, the bedroom lurching around her. Pain pulsed across the side of her face, like a physical thing. Like it had weight.

Beneath her touch, the dresser rattled.

Kevin snarled, the fur on his neck bristling like pine needles. "I've been nothing but good to you! Forget whatever shit Diane put into your head. We can forget about this. We'll go back to normal. We'll pretend this never happened. We'll be fine."

She touched the tender skin of her cheekbone. It was the hardest thing she had ever done, but she looked him in the eyes. She thought about the lake, about the light that sung and the shadow that saved her. She thought about her grandfather, who she never had enough time to hate. "Not this time, Kevin. It's over."

He lunged. She stumbled back, but he slammed his fist into her stomach and she crumbled, wheezing, tears pricking her eyes. He said something, but she couldn't hear it through the blood pulsing in her ears. He had always had a vicious streak, but she had never thought him capable of this. She had never thought his paws could hold this violence. She tried to scramble away, but he shoved her to the ground. He was on top of her then, one hand grinding her shoulder into the carpet, his minty breath coating her face like a virus, his heavy growling coming from somewhere deep within himself, somewhere she had glimpsed but never touched until now.

She clawed at his arms. It was desperate and stupid but it was *something*, and the thin lines of blood were like a candle in the dark. He hardly seemed to notice, slamming his fist into her again and again—shoulders, face, neck. Something cracked in her muzzle. She knew she was bleeding from the blood on his fist, stark against the golden fur, but all she felt was pain and panic. He was killing her. He was tearing her apart piece by piece, one painful fist at a time, until they did not seem to be separate blows but a continuous storm that howled and raged and ravaged her into nothing.

Through her blurry vision and the lurching room, she saw the mirror. But she did not see herself, just a swarming mass of shadows and claws, and she realized now that she could hear a distant howling wind, like a hurricane on TV. She locked gaze with two yellow eyes, slits so thin they were almost invisible.

Though she hurt so much she could hardly think, and though she was broken into a thousand pieces, she reached into the phoenix in her chest and found the strength to whisper, "Avizokal."

The world shattered. For a moment everything jolted and

glimmered and caught the light beyond the universe on silver-sharp edges like a glass dropped on hardwood floor. Then the world shifted back to normal, and a dark shape reached from the mirror. It grabbed the edges and heaved, ripples spreading across the surface as it pulled itself into the room. It was long and dark and jagged, like a charcoal nightmare sketched in the night. Yellow eyes bore into Kevin, who sat frozen above Sylvie with one fist still raised, his expression locked in terror.

Avizokal roared. It was like a storm slamming into the house. The windows shook, and the dresser rattled so hard a lamp shattered on the ground, and Kevin screamed. He lurched to his feet, drunk with horror, and bolted for the door. Avizokal was faster. Distant meant nothing to her—first she was in front of the mirror and then she was in front of him, swiping her claws down his chest. He screamed again and stumbled back, tripping over Sylvie. Blood welled onto his shirt. Avizokal loomed over him, slit eyes full of the fury of Hell, raising her jagged black claws for another strike.

Sylvie grabbed her leg. She felt fur, and up close she saw it was not just black but threaded with brown and red, like a darkened sky dusted with clouds. Avizokal looked at her, and even though Sylvie wanted to throw up and run away and never have to deal with any of this again, she managed to croak out, "Don't."

The demon lowered her claws. She crouched down, gently scooping Sylvie into her arms.

The next thing Sylvie knew, they were on the roof of the apartment building. She was not sure if she had blacked out or if they had simply gone from one place to the next. Kevin was gone. She closed her eyes tight and sucked in cool night air, letting her tears soak into the wiry fur of Avizokal's chest. Her body shook. Her heart pounded as if Kevin was still slamming his fist into her again and again, his eyes wide and rabid and desperate to keep his prey.

A rumbling hum in Avizokal's chest made her open her eyes. She could feel the sound inside her, the tune she had taught the demon. She tried to connect the shadow in the mirror to the creature before her. Moonlight traced an outline of a long snout and curving horns, like a dragon with black fur and goat eyes.

"You came," Sylvie managed to say.

Avizokal nodded, and then she went still as Sylvie reached up and traced a finger over her muzzle, from her slit nostril, along her lips, stopping at the soft fur of her cheek. When Sylvie showed no sign of fear, Avizokal closed her eyes and leaned her face into the otter's palm.

They stayed like that for a while, an otter and a demon and the cold night air, the world so still it felt like an insult to everything that had happened. Eventually Sylvie shifted, and Avizokal set her carefully on her feet, long-clawed hand more gentle on her back than Kevin had ever been. Sylvie was hurt and shaken and not entirely done with tears, but she leaned against Avizokal and saw that she had the strength to stand.

"Thank you," she said at last, aware of the wobble in her voice. "But you know, I don't think you're very good at this whole demon thing."

Avizokal chuckled in a rustle of leaves. Her eyes glowed in the moon.

Sylvie took a deep breath. "Okay. Alright. It's fine."

Avizokal rumbled.

"It'll *be* fine. Some day." She took another breath. The bird in her chest flared its wings, ready for anything, even as its flames flickered. She traced her thumb over the bottle cap in her pocket. She could do this. It would not be easy, but maybe she had the strength for it after all—the strength to reach out with all her heart and grasp on to what was real. "I don't suppose you remember where Diane's house is, do you? I need a phone."

Avizokal hummed from deep within her chest, picked Sylvie up into gentle arms, and pressed her lips briefly against the top of the otter's head. Then shadows filled the air, and they were gone.

Kary M. Jomb

Kary M. Jomb is a shadow mage who accidentally summoned a wormhole and slipped through it—like a water slide—into a twisted, sideways dimension where the animals talk, robots walk among us, and fairies hide in the flowers. She's working on a new spell that would let her transform into an otter. She loves otters, daffodils, sparkling water, and dark chocolate. Kary spends her time writing in coffee shops but doesn't drink coffee. She lives on the side of a hill in a liberal college town in the Pacific Northwest. She'd like to thank Mary E. Lowd for the opportunity to write in her universe.

SKY RIVER

The blue sun of Lottie IV glinted off the watery world's ice rings. Rocky chunks of diamond gleamed with sapphire light, stretched in a crescent across the world's pale sky. Its inhabitants—a long-spined, thick-furred, water-breathing, lutrinae species—had stared at that crescent of glittering ice from Lottie's oceans for generations. Out of reach. Unconquerable.

Today the rings would be conquered.

Rockets had seeded their sky with outposts and space stations. Over the last six decades, less than a lifetime, the Lottians had schemed and plotted to claim their birthright in the ice that had taunted their ancestors' dreams.

Today the ice would melt.

And Brunaia had the honor of pushing the final button— big, round, and red. Everything it should be. The stuff of legends, wired into a control panel on a space station, waiting for her to lower her paw. Her claws brushed against the button's smooth surface, and Brunaia's fur prickled all down her long spine, to the very tip of her rudder-like tail, with anticipation and liminal excitement.

Voices buzzed over the space station's comm-system:

"The heaters are ready," reported the general in charge of the fleet of spaceships used to position heating coils at regular intervals around the ring.

"A sufficient surface area of the ice fragments have been sprayed with glu-factor," reported the general in charge of the drone-ships for spraying glu-factor.

"Everything is ready," Brunaia said, and her voice was

carried to every Lottian in space around their world and most of the civilians planet-side. "Meltation now!" She pressed the button.

Heating coils buzzed to life and glowed a dull red, punctuating the arc of glittering diamonds that cut across the Lottian sky. For long moments, nothing else seemed to happen as the heating coils worked their magic, cutting into the ice. Frozen water boiled, molecules dancing away, captured by the vacuum of space. Then the glu-factor began to mix-in, calming and soothing the frantic molecules, pulling them together with massive surface tension. Droplets held, clinging to the ice chunks like sweat, grabbing onto each other, until BLOOP. The melted water hit a critical mass and glommed into a planet-wide ring. A looping river in the sky.

Lottians cheered all over their world, splashing for joy, as they watched their arc of ice wobble into a flowing sickle of shimmery fluid. Ice chunks still floated inside the sky-river, but they would melt soon.

"Install the water-locks," Brunaia ordered, and the general in charge of the water-lock gates relayed the message to her teams. Mechanical water-locks pierced the surface tension of the ever-flowing river, evenly spaced between the heating coils. Lottians would be able to use them to enter the river.

Finally, Brunaia ordered, "Release the fish."

From every water-lock, brightly colored fish spilled into their new home. All the colors of the rainbow swam in a translucent arc across the sky.

Joy filled the Lottians' hearts.

Brunaia took a deep breath and said, "I declare the Rainbow River open."

The blue light of the sun shone through the river as Lottians launched from the water-locks, carrying armfuls of kelp that streamed out behind them like green pennants.

Ryft Sarri

Ryft is a dog. He writes about this, that, and some otters, while trying to make some people laugh and more people think. A long time writer but new to the scene, he hides in the Pacific Northwest, learning more about writing every day and hoping for more rain. Maybe it will bring more otters.

CONVICTION

I don't know what to expect from my new friend's invitation.

I follow the super-powered student home all the same, growing slowly accustomed to the *swish-clump* noise of his every step. I've never known someone who wore boots like those before. Most kids I know barely even wrap their feet, let alone wear boots.

And he's so angry. Even when he was asking if I wanted to hang out after school, he was scowling. I'm also slowly growing accustomed to that, I think, as he talks. He's brimming with energy, and he focuses a lot of that into anger. Makes sense, I guess. I wonder why he seemed to attach to my greeting back in class.

We arrive, and he doesn't give me time to prepare before he opens the door and introduces me.

"It's good to meet you, Mr. and Mrs. Ramesen. I'm Max Vermillion, one of Hayden's new classmates."

The otters that greet me at my new raccoon friend's house come as a surprise. I get a nice smile of species familiarity from his mother. She looks kinda like *my* mom, but she definitely doesn't look like Hayden's. He was adopted, then. I bet she has powers too, so she could help Hayden get a handle on his. That would make sense.

"It's so nice to meet you! Imagine that, honey, our little Hay making a friend on his first day of hero classes." Hayden's dad is about an inch shorter than me and only a whisker taller than Hayden, but he definitely looks more like me than his own son. I wonder if we're related, distantly. Wouldn't that be funny?

I smile for them. "A guy like Hayden makes waves in our

little class. Being the resident water controller, I felt the need to dive in. Hayden said you were both doctors?" I play the polite house guest, just like I've been raised to do. Heroes must have manners, that's what I've been taught. Manners in this case means small talk, so I let them lead me to the living room where I sit on the couch with Hayden and answer questions about my family until they're satisfied. Then they talk about Hayden growing up and mention enough little details about his powers that I can piece together a general idea of what he can do.

"We always thought it was his powers that were the source of a lot of little Hay's anger problems. After they showed up, he was easier to upset and would just start glowing white when he did. All this energy started coming out of him in his fits." His mother smiles wistfully, like my mom does when she talks about me as a cub. "Oh, he used to break things when he threw a tantrum, all these tiny white explosions that would crack dishes or break lightbulbs. So you met Hay in the hero classes?"

Once his parents leave us to hang out in the living room, the raccoon on the other end of the couch sighs. "I thought they'd never shut up. They act like I've never had a friend over before."

"Just shows that they're interested. That's impressive for doctors." I've heard my dad say that before. I'm not really sure why it's all that impressive. Honestly, I'd like to agree with Hayden, but I'll have to be polite as the number one hero. Well-rounded and upright, that's what it takes to be at the top.

"Puh-leeze, they're *oppressive*, not *impressive*. All they do is nag me. Do your homework, do your chores, don't destroy the shed again. Like they think I don't know what I'm doing at a real school!"

Evidence of his homeschooling sits around us, begging me to contradict him. I have the sinking feeling that if I tried, I might see one of those explosions up close and personal. I don't think I'm quite ready for that. I need to see what he can do before I can confidently stand against him.

As if reading my mind, Hayden says, "We should spar. The rumor is you're the best in the class. I'd like to see what the best looks like."

My ears go back and I lose my smile for the first time since he invited me over. My nerves make a bit of water condense along the back of my neck. I smile back quickly and shrug. "I wouldn't want to hurt you or damage the house or property."

"Big sis has a healing power. Grandpa built the house to stand up to villain attacks." He counters my points without missing a beat. Then he turns those dagger sharp grey eyes on me. "You're not scared, are you?"

"No! I'm gonna be number one. I'm not scared of anything!" But he could see my lie. I pull my powers in on a tighter leash to dry off the sheen of water along my tail.

"Then prove it. Show me what it means to be number one." His stare is iron, and the words that follow seem typical of the top prospects from other schools. "Because I'm gonna be number one. You won't even make top ten." He has confidence when he says it, unlike my desperate proclamation.

"If your parents are okay with it, I guess." I mumble, then slink with him into the kitchen.

His folks seemed a bit more uptight than mine, but they're otter enough that when Hayden says, "Max and I are going to spar in the backyard. Send Liz out in about ten," they don't react beyond a few acknowledgements and a wave. From there I trudge through the sprawling ranch house behind the raccoon into what can only charitably be called a yard.

Battle scarred is the first phrase to come to mind when I see it through the sliding glass doors. The ground feels loose beneath me when I take my first step onto it, like it's been pulverized until it's almost sand in some places. Beside me, Hayden looks like he's settled into a better headspace. I can see the beginnings of a grin on his muzzle. "Stand over there and get ready. No blood, broken bones, and don't destroy the house or the fence. You get me?"

I blink at the raccoon, and the finger he's pointing across the yard. "Yeah, sure." I have that nervous feeling rising up in my gut again. The one that's right on the line between anxiety and fear. It twists my insides up until I feel like I'm going to puke, which nearly happens when I turn back to face Hayden.

Sure, I've had battle training and everything during Hero class—I'm actually pretty good at it. I have a solid handle on my powers and their application, and I only need to really work on making them stronger before getting my provisional license, just to make sure I have all my grounds covered. Against any first generation, I should have the advantage in a fight.

So why do I feel like I'm going to lose? The way that the world flows around him sends shivers down my spine and rattles my nerves.

Take a deep breath. Watch how he gets ready. You know his power, how do you think he'll use it? His mother told a lot of stories, but none of them were about fights, mostly just his temper. He's aggressive, though, and if he can use his power like an explosion, then he can launch himself at me. A charge is most likely, then, and he'll try and attack with a shockwave, since I don't know what to expect from them. I can evade wide just to be safe and counter attack. I wonder if he can use his power for defense. He wants to see what I can do too, so he'll probably back off and watch how I react before attacking again.

His paws come out of his pockets and I no longer have time for thinking that deep. A blast of white from the tips of his claws sends dust into the air and propels him straight at me, faster than I expected. I react as I planned, but I'm slow, slow, slow. I panic and summon water around my feet, letting me throw my center of gravity backwards and propel myself at the same time. *Counterattack* flashes through my head and I roll, pulling more water up to cushion my left paw so my right can fling a stream of it at the raccoon.

The only thing I succeed in doing is unbalancing myself. As I tip, my speed makes me lose control and I skid another foot before getting blasted with the outer edge of a massive white sphere. I clench my jaw and curl my rudder against my leg. *That* is pain. Oh, that is a lot of pain. I don't think, I only react. I throw my other arm towards where I think the attack is coming from and blast water towards it. No finesse, just as much water as I can push at him to put distance between us.

The pain lessens. I blink away the afterimage of the shockwave that I was hit with, only to find that my target is gone, and only a massive puddle behind where he was. I missed?

"You must be used to fighting that sorry bunch of middle schoolers. Try harder!" I whirl towards his voice and drop back to the ground immediately to avoid another white blast. I should have expected he'd be aggressive. What was I even thinking?

I really had been thinking he was just as predictable as the other students at my school. He clearly has far more experience. Backtrack, Max. General tactics. Hayden can take the high ground, metaphorically, due to his aerial maneuverability. I don't think I can win. He seems to be bending the world around him to his whim.

I have to try, though. I can't let him force me to give up. I shove myself up and twirl to my left to avoid another blast. Every opportunity I have, I'm hurling more water towards him, forceful streams to bump his trajectories and throw off his aim. I'm fighting purely defensively at this point. I don't have the honed reflexes that he does. I'm falling behind the flow of the battle.

I grit my teeth and push myself, straining to put more

power into every move than I have. I try to catch up with him, but Hayden is always one step ahead of me, dodging just out of my attacks a second before they reach him. *It's like he feels the tempo of the battle and can change it to suit him!*

This is what it takes to be number one. This is what I have to do if I want to compete. This is what I *need.*

The fight ends when Hayden leaps back, then rockets over my offense. With a snarled cry, he smashes through my attempt at defense and pins me to the ground by one shoulder. The way he moves using those shockwaves—he must have gotten his power really early on to be that comfortable with it. "You're too good. I can't beat you."

"Yet. I'm not too good, you're just not good enough. Work harder." He grins crookedly. "Until then, you're gonna be my sidekick." The jab is teasing, not serious, but it still has barbs.

For the first time in a long time, I bristle with anger at the thought. Sidekick? No, I'm going to be a *hero.* I'm going to be the best. This fight did exactly what I expect Hayden wanted it to. It was a kindness, in a rough, painful sort of way.

My anger is quelled when I see the fierce smile on Hayden's muzzle as he offers me his paw to get up. All of it is turned into a fierceness to compete with his. I match his smile and clasp his paw. In that touch, I feel the currents around us moving towards the future, a subtle shift in the atmosphere that makes my whiskers tingle. "That's better," he says. "Now you've got the eyes of a winner."

"And you sound like a lunatic," but I know he can tell that I don't mean it. We've gained that much of a kinship, just from that one spar. He really speaks a different language than I do, but I can feel us being drawn together and pushed forward by the currents of the world. I borrow some of his conviction, so that I can say, "But you're one hell of a fighter. Teach me how you learned to fight."

My dream is to be the number one hero, and now I won't let anyone stop me.

Madison Keller

Madison Keller is the author of the epic fantasy Flower's Fang series of fantasy novels and the humorous fantasy Dragonsbane Saga novella series as well as numerous short stories. His work has won both a Cóyotl and a LEO Award. A consummate dog lover and owner of two Chihuahuas, Otters are his favorite animal to see when visiting the aquarium because they are like the dogs of the sea. Madison makes his home in the Pacific Northwest, the land of otters. More information on Madison's writing can be found at www.MadisonKeller.net.

OTTER CHAOS

Shem dove down into the silty water, the headlamp on her head barely penetrating the gloom. Her light glinted off something in the mud, so she swam down to get a closer look. Her sleek form cut down like a knife, part of why she always felt more at home here than on land.

Her contact for this job had only given her an approximate location of the object he wanted retrieved from the riverbed. This job was like looking for a needle in a haystack, but that was why it would pay so well if she could deliver the goods.

Her air was running low, but the object was close. She angled down and dove for the glint. Bubbles escaped from her nose as she kicked her feet and steered with her tail. She used her hands to claw where the mud and silt sparkled in the lamplight.

The object was round and had some kind of logo on the side. It was a can from before the animals evolved, when the world's only sapient mammals were humans. Not what she was looking for, but valuable. She plucked it out of the mud and put it in her hip-pouch. This would be a nice bonus on an already lucrative job. If she could ever find the damn briefcase.

Her lungs screamed now. She twisted and planted her feet on the riverbed to push off towards the surface. Her whiskers broke through, and the cold night air made her shiver as the rest of her head bobbed above the water.

The sky was starting to lighten in the east, and she had to be out of here before she was spotted. This part of the river could be seen from the downtown waterfront park. It was always packed with bikers and joggers early in the morning, so she didn't usually scavenge here. Scavenging was considered looting, so those caught would face heavy fines and possibly jail time.

Still, she didn't want to come back tomorrow if she didn't have to. Despite the late hour, she decided she had time for one more run. After a big gulp of air, Shem dove back down. This time she swam downstream, trying to gauge the swirl of the unfamiliar currents and where they might have taken the case she was looking for.

The current led her to the bottom, and she dug down into the soft silt. At first, she only uncovered a few rocks as air bubbles escaped from her nose, counting down the moments until she had to ascend. Her claws scrapped on something hard, but softer than a rock. Digging further and faster, she uncovered the edge of a briefcase. It was one of the fancy, modern, aquatic designs, and it matched the description given to her by her contact. She kept digging until she found a handle that she could use that to lever it the rest of the way out. Her lungs screamed as she kicked and struggled to dredge the heavy case up.

Eats would be good this month with the payday she'd get for the briefcase. She wished the client had warned her about the weight, but then the client would need to know themselves what was in it.

Shem briefly wondered herself what was in it to make it so heavy, but pushed that thought out of her mind. It was dangerous to get involved. She didn't kid herself about who she was working for, about who would hire an unlicensed scavenger. It was better if she didn't know. Besides, with what she'd make from this job, she'd be able to afford her license and could start working on the right side of the law.

The dock on the east side of the waterfront was only about a foot off the water. Luckily, that was the side where the client had told her to call from. She paddled at the edge and hefted the case up and onto the dock, then scrambled up after it. She lay panting on the dock for a moment, letting her clothes air dry.

With short otter arms, she had to to half carry, half drag the heavy case along the sidewalk. It didn't get any lighter either as she walked ten blocks up east from the river. There was a coffee shop there that she knew would let her use their phone if she bought a pastry. The morning crowd was just trickling in by the time she arrived. She called the client's number while munching on a chocolate éclair.

A machine picked up, or maybe someone using a voice modulator, and gave her directions to a warehouse just a few blocks south of the coffee shop. She groaned and popped the rest of the éclair in her mouth, chewing as she walked out the door.

No one answered her knock at the warehouse's door. The voice hadn't given any instruction. Maybe she should go inside? She hesitated, knocked again, and waited. After another six breaths, she tried the doorknob. Unlocked. Huh.

She pushed open the door, dragged the case inside, and shut it behind her. "Hello?"

Only echoes greeted her. She sighed and set down the case. She wasn't leaving without getting paid, and she wasn't getting paid unless she could find the client.

There was an office in the corner with the light on. "I found your briefcase." No response came back.

She didn't really want to get her paw prints on anything here, but she wanted to get paid and gone. She opened the office door and was greeted by the badger who had hired her. Except now he had a big, bloody hole in his forehead.

Whatever was in this stupid case had better be worth it. She had hauled it all the way back to her apartment two miles away. Of course she'd tried to open it at the warehouse, but it had been locked too tight and she didn't want to stay there fiddling with it. She'd rifled through the badger's pockets, but they'd all been empty. Same with the office. Who knew when the badger's associate would show up to pay her, or if they'd think she killed him. Or, with her luck, the killer would show back up and kill her, too. No. Her contact was dead, so whatever was in the case was now her payday.

Shem's apartment was a studio, all she could afford on her inconsistent scavenging money. Her bed was in the corner furthest from the door, pushed up under the windows that overlooked the apartment building's courtyard. The long night of swimming and hauling the briefcase around had left her exhausted, so she crawled into bed right after getting home, still in her clothes. The briefcase handle felt like it was fused to her paw. She didn't even bother trying to pry it off, she just pulled the case into bed with her and fell asleep cuddling it.

The sound of splintering wood jolted her awake. She sat upright in bed and looked at her front door. It lay on the carpet, almost cracked in half down the middle.

Two wolves with guns drawn slunk inside, walking directly over her splintered door, their feet protected by thick combat boots designed for their back paws and hocks. Very expensive. They had to be custom made, since every mammal type had slightly different legs. It was the reason most people except for humans or the very rich went barefoot.

Her brain ran a million miles an hour, analyzing their expensive footwear, military grade guns, and flack vests while her muscles were frozen in place.

The two wolves turned to her, pointing their guns in her direction. "Freeze!" one of them growled.

Shit. Shem thought fast. She flung the case over her head at the window behind her, figuring it had to be what they were after. She was right. Their eyes widened, and the nearer wolf lunged towards the window, dropping his gun as he grabbed for the case. He was too far away and hit the carpet by her head with a thud that was covered by the sound of the cheap single-paned window shattering as the briefcase smashed into it. The second wolf kept his gun aimed at Shem, but his eyes followed the case. She took advantage of his distraction to scramble to her feet.

A few shards of glass had fallen on her bed and the window sill, but most had exploded outwards. She'd acted without thinking when she'd thrown the case out the window, she'd only wanted to distract them so that she could escape. But it hadn't worked, the wolves still stood between her and the only door. She lived on the fifth floor, so jumping out the window would be suicide.

That is, unless she could jump far enough to land in the pool that took up most of the courtyard below. That way, too, she could retrieve this briefcase that they were so obviously after. All this fuss, it had to have something valuable inside.

The wolf that had lunged towards her was getting to his feet, and that made her choice for her. She hopped up onto the window sill, cursing the bright sun that illuminated the courtyard and made it so she could see just how insane her plan was. Far, far below kids and adults of various species played in the pool. A few closest to her side had looked up and were pointing at her standing in the window. People yelled, but she couldn't make out what they were saying.

One glance at the yawning chasm between her and the ground far below made her reconsider. She yelped and turned her head to see the closer wolf grab for her. The morning sun glinted off his claws as he leered at her. She twisted her long, thin body away, and his claws grazed her side, slicing through her shirt and drawing four lines of blood.

Nothing for it then. Pretending in her mind that she was jumping off the high dive at the community pool, Shem leapt off the edge and into space, pushing out with her legs to try to get herself as far from the building as possible. She arched her back, pointed her arms down, and hoped she hit the water. Screaming followed her descent. She wasn't sure if it came from her or the spectators.

The relief she felt when her outstretched paws stung as they smacked into water instead of splatting on the concrete was short lived when a moment later her paws bounced off the bottom. She yelped and pulled them to her chest and twisted so that her shoulder hit the bottom next instead of her head. She relaxed her body, tucked her arms and head in, and floated for a moment. Her wrists both throbbed.

Paws grabbed her and pulled her to the surface and over to the pool's edge. Overlapping voices yelled in her ears, "Call an ambulance!" "What were you thinking, girl?" "Is she hurt?" "Watch out, there's another one!"

Her eyes popped open at that last statement and she looked up at her window. One of the wolves stood on the window ledge, crouching and preparing to jump.

"Shit!" Shem yelled, flailing her arms until her rescuers let her go. They looked at her, startled. Most of them were aquatic mammals like her, drawn to this apartment complex for the combination of cheap rent and a large pool. "He's after me," she explained to the crowd. "Ex-boyfriend that won't listen to me that it's over." That earned her more than a few sympathetic nods. "Can you buy me some time to get out of here?"

The wolf jumped. More screaming. The crowd helped her out of the pool and someone brought her the briefcase she'd thrown down earlier as the wolf landed with a huge splash.

"Here's your luggage!" She nodded her thanks and took it, nervously glancing at the water where the wolf had landed. He'd hit harder and was bigger than her. Blood stained the water in the shallow end where he'd landed. Shem looked away with a wince, closing her eyes.

Her wrists burned and ached holding the heavy case, but

she pushed through it and ignored the pain.

"Don't worry," one of the otter ladies said as Shem tottered forward. "We aquatics have to stick together, especially against larger animals like those wolves."

The mammals around her held up towels, shielding her from the view of the other wolf still upstairs and ushering her as a group to the parking lot. Her gaze was focused on the bus stop across the street when one of the group tugged on her arm.

"This way," the same otter women who had spoken to her before that she vaguely recognized from the hallways said. "I'll give you a ride wherever you need to go."

Shem almost cried in relief. "Thank you so much."

She crawled into the front seat of the other otter's car and put the case at her feet. Her wrists throbbed from carrying it just that short distance. Luckily, they were likely just strained. She doubted she'd be able to carry the heavy case at all if they were broken. She glanced in the rearview mirror as the woman started the car and drove out of the parking lot. The wolf was just climbing out of the pool, and it was obvious even at this distance that he'd broken one of his arms.

"Where can I take you?"

Shem gave her directions to a pawnshop on the other side of town that she knew would buy stolen goods. It wasn't one she normally frequented, to throw the wolves off. While the otter lady drove, Shem fiddled with the lock, but it was no good. The case was waterproof and high quality with a well-made lock. Without her tools, which were in her apartment, she wasn't getting it open.

Shem had the good-Samaritan otter drop her a block away in front of an apartment complex, telling the lady that she had a friend who lived at that apartment building who would hide her from her ex.

Shem regretted getting the woman involved. That wolf had caught sight of the back of her car, and she knew that they would come and question the lady to find out where she'd gone. Ideally, she would've had the woman drop her far away from anything. However, the state of her wrists meant that she wouldn't be able to carry the case very far. She needed to get it pawned and gone quickly. This was the best solution she could come up with.

Shem's wrists were screaming in agony by the time she got into the pawnshop. It hadn't helped that at first she'd had to pretend to ring her "friend's" apartment, because the good-Samaritan had insisted on waiting until she was safe inside. Shem had rung random apartments until someone buzzed her inside. She then waited for a count of one-hundred before leaving and making her way to the pawnshop.

The big bull moose behind the counter snorted and gave her a very short once over. She held her head high, her thick tail trailing behind her as she waddled up to the counter in front of the moose. The top of it was over two feet taller than her. He didn't say anything, but lifted his arm and pointed a hoof-tipped finger to his left, around the corner of his counter at something she couldn't see. Shem's wrists were giving out, so she set down the case and waddled over so she could peer around it.

A smaller, lower wooden counter about two feet tall was there to serve smaller mammals, staffed by the tiniest dog that Shem had ever seen. At least she thought it was a dog. He wore a vintage black band shirt and had huge ears lined in fluff with a big shock of white hair between them, big round eyes, a hairless face, and a short, thin muzzle. He looked up at her from his seat. The moment he saw her, the whip-thin tail edged in a white plume that curled up behind his back began wagging furiously.

"Hello, hello!" he called, gesturing one surprisingly furry paw to beckon her forward. "I can help you here."

"Um, be right there." Shem said. With a groan she plodded back to the case and dragged it over. "I have this case to sell."

"Just the case?" he asked as she levered it up onto the counter in front of the dog. "It looks heavy. Is it empty?"

"No, there's something inside it." The case taken care of, she sagged forward, half-lying, half-standing against the front of the counter.

"Let's see here." The little dog reached out to slide the case around until the lock was facing him. He pulled a pair of glasses off the top of his head that she hadn't seen in the shock of white fluff and perched them on his muzzle. They made his already huge eyes look even larger as he leaned forward to peer at the case. "Oh, yes. Wonderful," he muttered quietly to himself, then his voice raised to address her, although he didn't glance up at her. "Quality brand. Favored by aquatics such as yourself to keep your possessions dry during underwater trips. It's a little scuffed up, but only superficial damage."

Shem perked up at his words despite her still-shaking paws. Maybe she wouldn't be out too much on this job after all. "How much can I get?"

The dog glanced up briefly at her before flicking his eyes back down to the case. "Not sure yet. I'll let you know when I finish my examination." He reached a paw up and tugged at the clasps. When it didn't open he pushed at the lock, and then leaned back and took off his glasses to look at her. "It's locked."

"I know. I found it while scavenging, so I don't have the key. Can you still take it?" Shem started to wring her paws together nervously, but stopped when they twinged painfully.

The dog shook his head, placing his glasses back on top of his head between his ears. "Look, otter, we don't ask many questions, but you need to at least make an effort to *pretend* these things aren't stolen."

"But I didn't—"

The dog stood and yipped, cutting her off. "Roscoe, kick

her out."

The moose only had to take one step to get over the tiny counter. Over her increasingly loud protests he picked up the briefcase in one hand, her in the other, and marched them both out of the shop's backdoor. He dumped both her and the case in the alley next to the dumpster before strolling back inside.

Shem lay in that alley for far too long, trying her best to pick the damn lock on the case, but it was hopeless. That dog had been right; the case was top quality, and it came with a lock to match. Even if she had her tools, she estimated it would take days to break in. And she didn't have days before those wolves tracked her here. Without knowing what was in the case, she couldn't try to sell it to her usual contacts. She had limited options.

Raised voices from inside drew her attention. Shem left the case lying on the ground and stood, moving to press one short, round ear against the back door.

"This isn't the Brahman's territory. We don't answer to you and we don't divulge information about our clients." The moose's rumbling bass was easy for even her poor otter hearing to pick up.

A loud growl came in response, too low pitched to have come from the tiny dog. "The otter came through here, I can smell her. Where's the case?"

Shem backed away from the door in alarm. That growl, being able to smell her, asking about the case, they all added up to the wolves having found her. She was out of time.

Where could she go to get away from them? Her contact for the job was dead, and she didn't know who *he'd* worked for, so she couldn't go to the source. Her apartment was already compromised.

Shem cradled her head in her paws and stifled a groan. She put her paws down and began to pace, trying to think.

Something crackled in her pocket at her hip. She opened it and pulled out the old can. In all the excitement of finding the briefcase, she'd forgotten about it. The can was valuable; the pawnshop would take it for sure. Then, she could buy tools to open the case and figure out why everyone wanted it so badly.

She glanced back at the door she'd been thrown out of. Well, maybe not this pawnshop. Good thing downtown Portland was filled with them. There was another one she knew of around here. Picking up the case, Shem waddled away as fast as she could. After just a block, not just her wrists, but also her biceps ached from lifting it up high enough not to drag. She caught sight of a tent three or four blocks up the street. Wait, was today Saturday? The Saturday Market would have someone willing to trade her tools for the can.

The sun was starting to set, and the people in the tents would be packing up soon. Shem forced herself to pick up the pace but only had made it a dozen paces when two wolves stepped out of the alley in front of her. Wolves she recognized from her apartment. One had his arm in a brace and strapped to his chest. They both glared at her and bared their teeth.

Shit. She couldn't run. Even if she hadn't been lugging the heavy case, the wolves would have been able to easily catch her.

"Give us the case, girl," the uninjured one growled, "and we might let you live."

Shem narrowed her eyes and hissed at them. "No."

The wolves didn't give any warning, they just charged forward at her as one at some unspoken signal, snapping their jaws at her.

Shem let out a bark of surprise, tightening her grip on the case. On instinct she swung it around, using her thick tail to balance as the heavy case flew. It slammed into the face of the first wolf with a satisfying thwack. He dropped like a sack of bricks to the pavement, unconscious. The case bounced off and Shem changed directions, swinging it towards the other advancing wolf who flinched back, shielding his broken arm as she continued her pirouette. The wolf had been moving too fast, and by the time he skidded to a stop he was in the path of the case's continued rotation. The side of the case smashed into his lower leg with a crunch. The wolf fell, screaming and clutching at his leg. She winced. She hadn't really wanted to hurt them, only to give herself enough time to get away.

"Sorry," Shem called, continuing to spin with the momentum of the heavy case. Her wrists and shoulders screamed at the abuse, but she didn't dare let go and possibly lose it. The whirl brought her back around, where the case smacked into the screaming wolf's head. It made a pinging sound and popped open. Paper documents, photos, data disks, and, of all things, a gun, tumbled out onto the street. The wolf's eyes rolled back and he mercifully stopped screaming, falling prone to the pavement.

Shem grabbed for the closest papers, frantically stuffing them back into the case. The entire fight had taken less than thirty seconds, but the wolf's screams had drawn attention from the merchants at the closing market and she could hear and see people headed her way.

Luckily most of the contents had stayed in the case, so it only took her a few moments to grab what had come out. Shem used one of the documents to grab the gun and drop it back into the case. No reason to get her paw prints on it. She tried to shut it when she was done, but the lock wouldn't catch. Shem held it closed with both paws and carried into the alley the wolves had come out of. Halfway down was a storm drain with bars that looked wide enough for her sleek form to slide through, but close enough together that most other mammals would have a hard time following her. She ducked down it and hid at a bend in the tunnel. Voices called back and forth about getting the wolves an ambulance. A few of them mentioned seeing a third person, but most of the onlookers had apparently mistaken her for a large weasel or martin from the distance, so she wasn't worried if even someone did spot her.

Once it was clear no one was going to find her here, she ignored the commotion outside and began rifling through the contents of the case. Since she didn't have a laptop or other way to see what was on the data-discs, she ignored those and the gun, and focused on the papers and photos.

The photos were disturbing scenes of graphic torture. Once she figured out what was going on in them, she didn't look too closely. Each picture showed different victims, but the perpetrators were always the same two mammals. A big brown cow with a hump and a bison.

She didn't recognize their faces, but she knew who they were by reputation. The Brahman cow was one of the city's top crime bosses. The police hadn't been able to pin anything on her directly, and she was always let off due to lack of evidence. The bison with her was one of her enforcers. Shem started to shake as she threw the photos back in the case.

The photos alone were damning enough evidence, but the documents were even worse. They detailed the Brahman's orders to associates, including print outs of emails and copies of business contracts. The fading light made it hard to read too much, but it didn't really matter since she didn't understand the significance of most of them anyway.

No wonder those wolves had been so hot to get the case from her, and she hadn't even looked at the data-discs. Not to mention the gun.

Shem was sure the Brahman would pay a fortune to get this back. She even knew a way she could make contact, through one of the shadier pawn shops that lined the east side of the river. She was already going through plans in her head about where she could stash the briefcase while she set it up. She turned to put the pages back when one of the photos caught her eye, because the face of the mammal being tortured was familiar.

She picked it up and waddled closer to the grate, holding it up to see it better in the dim sunset light. She put a paw over her mouth to stifle a sob when she realized who it was—a river otter, like her, who she used to frequently see in the evenings as she prepared for scavenging runs. His name was Melvin, and he ran boat tours of the Willamette River for tourists. She hadn't seen him or his boat for the last few months, but had figured that his schedule had changed.

In the picture Melvin's handsome face was twisted up in fear and pain, his mouth open in a scream as the bison held a red-hot poker against his side. His once-silky brown fur was matted and stained with streaks of blood, and one of his eyes was nothing more than a red pit. The Brahman was in the corner of the photo. Both she and the bison were smiling.

Shem lowered the picture and shuffled back to drop it in the case. She shut it, the sat down on the top and stared at the inside of the storm drain until she could no longer see it. He couldn't have survived those injuries. They'd killed him. Not just that, but they'd enjoyed it.

What else could she do? No one else was able to stand up to the Brahman, not even the police had been able to stop her. But then again, they didn't have what was in this case. All this direct evidence of the cow's crimes.

Shem sat there all night on top of the case, thinking, and by morning she knew what she had to do.

Shem had been in this room for either one entire century or only a few minutes. Without clocks or windows, and with her complete exhaustion causing her to keep nodding off in the uncomfortable chair, only to jerk awake again an unknown amount of time later, it was hard to measure time. Finally, she woke for the umpteenth time to find a beaver in a suit coat and slacks sitting in the chair across from her. Shem lifted her cuffed paws up to wipe the sleep gunk from her eyes before straightening to watch the beaver fiddle with a file folder that she'd placed in front of her on the table.

"Hello, I'm Detective Digger." The beaver let go of the papers and clasped her webbed paws on top of the folder. "You are Shem, correct?"

Shem just blinked for a moment, and then gave a quick nod of her head. To Shem's surprise, the beaver looked relieved.

"Excellent. We've been trying to track you down since the undercover officer who hired you was found murdered."

"The badger?" Shem blurted in surprise. "He was a cop?" The beaver nodded, and a lot of things clicked into place. "I came here voluntarily, gave you all that evidence, and now I hear I was working for you to start with," Shem rattled the cuffs against the ring on the table that they were threaded through, "so what's with these?"

The beaver sighed and shook her head. "That cow always seems to be one step ahead of us, and—"

"You needed to be sure it wasn't a set up?"

Detective Digger nodded once. "Exactly. We're busy setting up a safe house where you can stay until the trial, since your place is compromised."

Shem's mind whirled. She hadn't thought that far ahead. "Trial? Why do you need me there? You have all that evidence."

"Of course, but we need you to testify about where it came from, prove that we didn't obtain it illegally," the beaver waved a webbed paw, "and all that. With what you brought us, we'll be able to put away one of the biggest crime bosses in the city. We've been trying to nail that Brahman bastard for murder for years, but she keeps slipping through our paws. Not this time."

Shem yawned, struggling to keep her eyes open. She hadn't known she'd have to testify. But then Melvin's face from the picture came back to her. She would do whatever she could to keep the Brahman from doing that to anyone else. "Where did it all come from, anyway?"

"A member working for her organization gathered physical evidence for us from the Brahman's office." She tapped the table. "He was trying to get his family out from under the cow's big hooves. He got attacked on the way to deliver the evidence to his contact, the badger who hired you. The informant managed to ditch the case in the river as he ran, but he was gunned down before he could get away."

"Why hire me?" Shem frowned. "I mean, you're a beaver! You could have swum down there yourself and gotten it. Or any of the aquatics on the force."

The beaver shook her head. "Too many leaks. We didn't know who was on the Brahman's payroll. Even any of the licensed scavengers could have been working for her. It had to be someone outside, someone underground who was too far beneath the cow's notice for her to bother bribing."

Shem slumped in her seat at the description of herself, but couldn't argue with its accuracy. "But she still found out, didn't she? That why the badger was dead when I went to collect payment."

Detective Digger nodded. "Exactly. She must have sent men to retrieve the evidence from our undercover agent, not realizing that it had taken you longer than anticipated to find the briefcase."

"Hey now," Shem growled, sitting her long spine up straight and thrashing her thick tail hard enough to rock the metal chair she sat in. "The location given to me was a huge area! And I could only work at night!"

The beaver held up her webbed paws in a gesture of surrender and gave Shem a broad smile. "Not faulting. I know how hard it is to see in dark, murky water. Actually, now that we're on the subject..." She pointed both index fingers down to the cuffs on Shem's wrists. "Let's get those off of you." She pulled a key out of her jacket pocket and leaned across the table to put it into the cuffs.

While she fiddled with the lock, the beaver kept talking. "We'd like to offer you a job."

"A job?" Shem repeated in shock. That was about the last thing she expected the beaver to say. "As a detective?"

The second cuff came off and Shem sat back, rubbing her wrists, still sore from her slam into the bottom of the pool earlier that day. Or yesterday. Whenever.

Detective Digger shook her head, giggling slightly as she sat back. "No, no. As a police diver. Retrieving evidence that land mammals think they can get rid of by tossing it in the Willamette or Columbia, or any of the thousands of lakes dotting the area. But if it is detective work you are interested in, I'd be happy to write you a letter of recommendation to the police academy."

Shem blinked. "Police academy? Oh, uh, no, I, uh, a diving job is great. I love swimming, but I don't have a license..." Her head swam. A real job. Regular income? She never thought she'd see the day.

The beaver waved a paw. "We'll take care of it." She stood and stuck her hand out across the table. In a daze, Shem reached out and shook it. "Welcome aboard," Detective Digger said happily.

Frances Pauli

Frances is the author of numerous speculative fiction novels including the Leo Award winning, Earth Tigers. She very much enjoyed frolicking with the otters for this story, and promises she hasn't secretly taken any home with her even though they would fit in well with her menagerie of houseplants, serpents, hairless dogs, and tarantulas. She dwells in the less rainy, inland portion of the Pacific Northwest and can be found writing animal stories ninety percent of the time.

OTTER DANCE

The doumbek pounded a heartbeat rhythm and the hafla crowd trilled their tongues against the roofs of their mouths. Feet stamped in time to the drum. Incense burned beside the stage, a pungent copal smoke that tickled Arina's nostrils and threatened to make her sneeze.

Not what she needed right before a performance.

The troupe gathered behind the curtain, two minks, a ferret, a stoat, and Arina. They wore matching saffron skirts and choli tops, and each dancer had circled her hips in a wrap dripping with copper coins and jangles. The music started. The doumbek paused its beating.

The crowd hushed in anticipation of the dance.

Arina had memorized every step of the routine. She'd practiced with the troupe for weeks and at home every night by herself. The otter's heart still pounded in her chest. When the familiar notes of the baladi signaled their cue to enter, her nerves felt like fire, sharp and electric.

The minks led the way, swirling onto the stage in a flutter of silk. The ferret and the stoat followed, and then Arina moved in behind them. The pipes whined and the weasels all undulated, snakelike for the crowd. Behind them, towering over them, Arina moved her hips and shoulders in an imitation that somehow always manage to end up too bouncy.

Her bones were too rigid. Her webbed paws made a clunky noise as the troupe shifted positions across the stage. When it was her turn to move to the front, her furry body nearly eclipsed the others.

Arina padded forward, rolled her hips sharply from one

side to the other, and moved her arms in a too-stiff imitation of snakes writhing. She shuffled back again, letting the others refill the gap, counting each beat in her mind. One, two, three, four. Her body shimmied, and the stage shook.

The rest of the troupe jingled like the rain falling, their belts matching time to the quicker rhythm. Arina twisted at her waist and her coins clanked together, as heavy as her rudder-like tail.

Their dance led them in a serpentine from one side of the stage to the other, and each dancer took her turn winding back and forth between the others. Arina used her tail to help her pivot, but nearly tripped Jayla, the group's leader, as they exchanged places. When they passed the next time Jayla's stage smile cracking into a snarl.

Arina pretended she hadn't seen it. She moved to the front again, attempted to spin without her tail's assistance and wobbled to one side, nearly bumping one of the other girls and barely keeping her feet. Her cheeks flamed in embarrassment.

In the audience, a sea of furry faces watched the dance. Ears pricked and swiveled to catch the music. Arina could see them over her fellow dancers. She could see each wince when her paws came down, could see them cringing when her coins drowned out the jingling of the others.

With her face alfame, the otter executed her routine, flawlessly, without misstepping once. With her heart sinking, she finished, following the troupe in a swirl of saffron silk, off the stage and back out, into the smoke.

Arina watched the tribal soloist from the rear of the audience. The otter still wore her costume, but had donned a colorful caftan cover-up and then wandered between the vendor's booths before settling in to watch the rest of the performers. She sat near the back, and in the darkened theater, hadn't noticed her own troupe in front of her until Jayla, a satiny mink, spoke.

"Emilia wants to join us." Jayla's tiny ears twitched forward and back. She leaned over and pressed her muzzle close to the others. "She's been dancing for six years."

"Is she any good?" Osi, the ferret, leaned across Mia and Lao. "What's she dance like?"

"She's an ermine." Jayla made the word *ermine* into a declaration, as if the girl's species would automatically convey her skill.

Arina sat back in her chair. She'd meant to speak up, to let them know she was there, in the dark behind them. But the tone of their voices brooked secrecy, and that word, *ermine*, echoed in her much larger ears. This new girl was a weasel, too.

"We can't add anyone else," Mia shrugged her silky shoulders. "We'd have to re-choreograph everything."

"It wouldn't be that hard," Osi said it, but the way her voice lingered in the air gave the words a nasty vibe.

Arina's fur prickled along her spine.

"Maybe we wouldn't have to, if..." Jayla trailed off. She didn't finish her sentence, but judging from the others, she didn't have to. They all lowered their noses, hunching forward as if the guilt of their topic weighed down on them.

A chill crept from Arina's rudder tail to her round head. This wasn't the first time they'd had this conversation, was it? Her chest tightened, as if she'd been underwater a moment too long and needed to surface. She breathed, but the air felt thin and weak in her lungs. Clutching the front of her caftan closed, she tried to stand and ease her way out of the aisle.

The jingle belt gave her away. Her coins clanked as she twisted between the seats and four pointed, fuzzy faces turned to stare at her with too-wide eyes. Arina saw them through a blur. She tried blinking, twisted to free herself, and then shuffled her big, webbed feet. Her tail pinched in the small space, but her heart beat, frantic to get away.

Almost all of them had been shocked to see her. Arina freed herself, knocking and clanking her way loose and then practically diving through the back doors. All but one. She hugged her caftan tight as she ran. In her mind's eye she saw Jayla's expression, a smug twist of the mink's muzzle, the flash of triumph in her beady eyes.

She'd known exactly who sat behind them. She'd done it on purpose, and now... Now nothing in the whole of the world would drag Arina back to practice. Jayla had won. The troupe would have their ermine, and she...

The otter sniffled. She slid to a stop just outside the theater's rear entrance. The night air was biting cold, quiet, but she could still hear the muffled beat of the doumbeks, the drums that sounded distant now, too far off to reach. The ermine would move like a snake to that beat. She'd suit them. She'd match and ripple and never eclipse another dancer with her bumbling body.

Arina listened in the darkness, alone. Her hips swayed once, when the beat quickened, but she tamped down the urge and let the tears fall freely. Her big shoulders shook and her stout, otter arms hugged her caftan to cover herself as if even wearing the costume were somehow shameful.

She should have stuck to swimming. Should have known an otter wasn't made for grace, for music. Arina nodded to no one in particular and sighed. The troupe could have their ermine and *she* would never dance again.

"So you just quit?" Mella sat on the bank, swishing her strong rear legs through the water and leaning back on her paws to eye the blue sky above.

"Well, sort of." Arina swam to the riverbank and pulled herself out. She shook, dislodging a rain of huge droplets and soaking her friend all over again.

The capybara cringed and held up both front paws. "Cut it

out. What do you mean, sort of?"

"I mean I *sort of* just stopped going to practice." Arina sighed and flopped onto her belly. Her tail tip still dragged in the water, tugged softly by the river's leisurely current. "What was I supposed to do?"

"I'd have told them all where to stuff it." Mella huffed, full of bravado when there was no one to actually call her on her bluff. "I never liked them."

"Well, I thought I did." The sting of her troupe's rejection was still fresh enough to make Arina growly. Thankfully, Mella didn't notice. The capybara girl had a gravelly voice, and today it was full of indignation for Arina's benefit.

"We should go down there and throw rocks at them."

"I'd rather just stay here and swim."

"But you *loved* dancing." Mella sighed and kicked her hind paws, splashing the water into a sparkling froth.

"I don't really want to talk about it."

"Sorry." Mella hunched her shoulders and turned her huge, squarish head in her friend's direction. She had bristly hair compared to the otter, a blunt nose and a squat body, but her eyes were soft and as kind as a bunny's. If she acted fierce now, it was in defense of her friend, and that alone took some of the gloom from Arina's mood. "Do you want to swim some more?"

"Yep."

The otter grinned and pushed herself back into the cool flow. Her webbed feet threshed the water while Mella splashed in, and she drifted downstream a few paces to wait for the capybara to get paddling. They swam with their heads high above the water, as lazy as the river today. The sun cast diamonds along the ripples. It warmed Arina's fur, and she ducked under and used her tail to drive her across to the far bank and back.

When she surfaced, Mella let out a grunt, splashing water toward Arina with her front paws. "Show off."

"Just getting cool. It's hot today."

"Yeah, it is." The capybara dipped her nose toward the river's surface, but stopped short of putting her face in the water. She paddled hard, constantly moving all four paws to stay afloat. Her breath already huffed from the exertion, but she swam a little circle against the current, ears flicking and chin just resting on the water.

Arina could have swam all day. Her friend tired much faster, however, and for Mella's sake, she shook off the urge to dive, to streak upstream and then roll over and float all the way back down. "Let's go get lunch."

"You sure?" Mella's voice gave away her eagerness. She turned for the shore before Arina had voiced her answer.

"Yeah." Arina stroked her tail from side to side and streaked past her friend. The cool water flowing over her fur felt delicious, almost better than the beat of a doumbek pounding low and steady. She reached the bank, climbed out and shook before Mella made it to shore.

The river babbled while they dried and dressed. A few birds sang in the distance. The otter smoothed her sleek fur and listened. She closed her eyes, let the sun warm her whiskers, and swayed her hips softly from one side to the other.

"Aren't you going to go?" Arina's mother set down a tray of fish and gazed across the table with concern crinkling the corners of her eyes. "Jayla's mother said it was the biggest hafla of the season. All the girls are going."

Arina hunched over her plate. She stabbed a piece of her fish and twirled it on the end of her fork. Her mother had taken the news of her leaving the dance troupe less well than she'd hoped. That she was still talking with Jayla's mom, suggested she believed the girls would patch things up. As usual, her mother had missed the entire point.

"I don't really want to."

"Well, that's just fine isn't it?" The elder otter sniffled too loudly to be authentic. "Six months ago, all you wanted to do was dance. Couldn't get you in the pool if we tried. Six months of running you back and forth to practice, of nothing but jingling coins and, and... Walter, you tell her."

Arina's dad jerked in his seat as if he'd been startled awake. His head came up slowly, mouth chewing on his latest bite of fish. He stared across the table, swallowed before answering. "What's that dear?"

"Arina doesn't want to go to the hafla."

"I thought she quit dancing?"

"Exactly." Her mother crossed her arms and glared at her as if anything her father had said supported her argument by default. "And Siradi is going to be there. You've got no less than six pictures of her in your room, young lady, and now you don't want to go?"

"I—"

"I've already bought us all tickets." That tone ended the discussion. It left no room for argument, not that Arina had been prepared to continue. She didn't want to see Jayla and the girls again, but Siradi she *did* want to see. At least she had when she still dreamed of being a dancer.

"May I be excused?" Arina kept her voice quiet, her eyes down. She'd finished half of her fish, and just looking at the rest of it made her stomach flip-flop. "Please?"

"I suppose." Her mother squinted at her, tightened her whiskers, and then sighed loudly enough that Arina's father jumped again. "But we're not done talking about this."

"Okay." She pushed her chair back and snatched up her plate, scampering with it to the kitchen sink and then high-tailing it for her bedroom. Once safely ensconced there, Arina flopped onto her bed and rolled to her back. She stared at the ceiling, and Siradi stared back at her.

The honey badger had won the international bellydance

finals two consecutive times. She had her own line of instruction videos, several of which Arina owned, and there were nine posters of the dancer in Arina's room. Her mother had obviously never bothered to count.

"I can't dance," Arina told her hero. "I'm big-boned, graceless, uncoordinated."

On the ceiling, the poster version of Siradi smiled as if the world were watching. She held her arms over her head, zills tapping tightly between her fuzzy fingers. Her costume blurred, caught forever in mid-swirl. One of her feet was visible beneath the skirt, half cocked and ready to take the next step.

Arina could hear the music, just looking at the image. She could feel it, deep in the center of her belly. She rocked from side to side with the imaginary rhythm. It didn't mean she couldn't go watch. Just because she wasn't cut out to dance, didn't mean she couldn't see Siradi, at least this once. If she ran into Jayla and the girls, she could always pretend her mother had forced her to come. She could tell them she was so over dancing.

In her fantasy, she sighed, deliciously bored sounding, and explained that she'd completely lost interest in bellydance. She rolled her eyes while their tiny jaws dropped open. *I've moved on,* daydream Arina drawled. *I'm looking for something a little more interesting.*

After they'd run away sniffling, Arina imagined she would give a final little twirl in homage to their tedium. She'd end with a flourish, in exactly the same pose Siradi adopted, and just as her skirts swirled about her ankles, a soft applause would erupt behind her. She'd turn, shocked to find the honey badger herself had been watching. While Siradi praised her, begging her to enroll in her personal classes, Jayla and the troupe would return to witness Arina's humble protests....

Her bedroom door shuddered under her mother's signature knocking. "Arina?"

She sat up, blinking away the daydream. "Yes?"

"I've gotten enough tickets that you can bring Mella if you like. Make sure she asks her mother."

"Okay." She waited until footsteps drifted away from the door before flopping back into her pillows again. Having Mella along would help. She felt like she could brave the hafla with her best friend in tow. Then again, the capybara could end up witnessing her humiliation, too.

Arina imagined again, and this time, the daydream ended with her tripping over her own feet, with the old troupe laughing at her while her family and her best friend stood by and watched. She shouldn't go at all. That was it. She didn't want to.

But when she looked up at the honey badger on her ceiling, all Arina could do was imagine dancing again.

The theater had sold out the day after her mother bought them all tickets. The parking lot was full, and a big sandwich board had been set outside the doors, painted with a flourishing border and the words *Hafla Oasis*.

They'd picked Mella up on the way, and as soon as Arina's dad squeezed their car into the space, the capybara had unbuckled herself and bounced out of the vehicle. Arina had less luck feigning enthusiasm. Her legs trembled, and she'd spent the entire ride to the theater imagining horrible ways to be embarrassed by Jayla and company.

Her latest terror ended with her on her rump, surrounded by a ring of weasels and one, wholly unimpressed, famous honey badger.

Her parents led the way with Mella scampering behind them and Arina shuffling at the rear. A tall coyote in a pair of harem pants took their tickets. He grinned at the girls, winked one yellow eye and flashed his plume tail back and forth against the purple silk bottoms. When Arina's mother asked

him for directions to their seats, he pointed both with his paw
and his ears, toward the center of the theater seats.

The lights were up. Arina scanned the faces to the front
and back this time. She found no one she recognized, so she
squeezed into the aisle with a slightly reassured heart. Mella
filled the seat to her left, and the row to their right was still
empty. The panic returned as she imagined Jayla's family
sitting there, as she wondered how far their parents had gone
in their attempt to mend fences.

When a family of skunks scooted in to take the remaining
seats, Arina exhaled a measure of nerves and let her head rest
back against the velvet seat.

"Are you okay?" Mella whispered. The capybara's bristly
hair tickled Arina's ear.

"Why wouldn't I be okay?" The sharpness of her voice
lowered her muzzle. "Sorry."

"It's all right. I bet they're no good anyway."

"No." Arina tucked her paws into the cracks at the sides of
her seat. "They're going to be wonderful."

She stared at the back of a round, graying head, a possum
sitting in the next row forward. When Mella muttered
something under her breath, Arina found herself feeling
defensive for the troupe. Weirdly enough, she hoped they were
wonderful. In all her daydreams, she'd never once imagined
that her troupe would dance poorly. It had always been about
her, one way or the other.

She didn't want them to fail. She wanted them to want her
back.

The lights lowered briefly, signaling for the stragglers to
take their seats. Mella shifted back and forth, getting
comfortable by wiggling deeper into the velvet cushion as if she
could burrow in. A rustling of fur and fabric filled the huge
theater as all the remaining animals worked their way between
the aisles to sit. Voices lowered, eventually hushed, and the

lights were lowered again, this time, to leave the immense room in darkness.

From just off stage, a doumbek thumped. A high-pitched pipe whined and warbled over the steady rhythm of the drum. The big curtain drifted open, a sweeping of heavy fabric in the dark. Behind it, a spotlight flared. Low bulbs along the front of the stage ignited, casting the curtain's shadow across the boards.

The music lifted. A line of musicians danced in, wild, uncoordinated dancing that succeeded in fixing the audience's attention forward. The drummers spun, hunched over doumbeks held tightly between bent knees. A flautist and a piper dodged between them, weaving the line and serenading the audience with a squealing melody. The coyote in purple harem pants held a smaller drum, beating it with his free palm in a tapping, higher staccato.

Offstage, the dancers trilled. A few of the knowing audience members joined in, and the musicians encouraged the gesture with wilder dancing and faster music. A few people tried clapping along, but the trilling swelled and won over the rebels.

By the time the musicians faded to the rear of the stage, taking up positions on pillows and fabric draped stools, the whole theater echoed with reverberating appreciation. Arina leaned forward in her seat. Her paws tapped softly in time to the beat. When the song ended, the trilling faded away. Quiet returned, as if the entire theater held their breaths.

The lighting shifted toward the front of the stage, casting the musicians into a shadowy background. A single note howled from one pipe, but it was enough to tell Arina who the first act would be. She'd practiced to that sound often enough. When the drums jumped in she sat back, stuffed her paws under her thighs, and closed her eyes.

Mella leaned closer, whispering. "It's them."

Arina nodded. She had to look then or Mella would know how embarrassed she felt, how her pelt wanted to crawl from her bones and hide beneath her seat. She opened her eyes as the notes of the baladi filled the theater. Jayla and the others undulated across the stage, and instead of an enormous otter in their midst, a snow-white ermine took her place.

It really did suit them better.

Sitting out here, surrounded by darkness, it was much easier to be objective. The ermine moved the same way the others did. She flexed like a ferret, undulated like a mink, and stepped on tiny weasel paws. Dainty and graceful and never clanking once.

"They look lovely together." She meant the statement for herself, a private observation that slipped through her lips.

Mella grunted. "The white one keeps messing up."

"What?" Arina sat back in her seat when the possum in front of her turned and gave her a dirty look. She whispered, hoping Mella would follow suit. "What do you mean?"

"The white one is doing the wrong steps." The capybara lowered her voice, but not enough to keep Arina's face from heating. She said it with triumph in her voice, enough for Arina to suspect she was just defending her.

Except she was right. When Arina looked again, she noticed the fumbles. She'd been so impressed by the sinewy undulations of the weasels—and the ermine's undulations were flawless—that she'd missed the new girl's stutters. When the troupe turned next, the ermine spun in the wrong direction.

"She hasn't had enough time to learn the choreography," she said. "No one could have had it down that fast."

"Sure." Mella didn't sound convinced. She sounded glad that the ermine was struggling.

Arina couldn't feel anything but sorry for the girl. She knew exactly what it was like to be self-conscious on stage, and for all her chunkiness, she'd always at least gotten the steps right. The ermine hadn't had time to learn the routine, and it didn't seem fair at all to expect perfection from her.

"Poor thing," she whispered.

Mella snorted as if it were only justice, as if the ermine girl had been responsible for Jayla's action. Not right. Arina cringed when the white weasel fumbled a step again. She moved beautifully, danced just like the others. If they gave her enough of a chance, she'd blend in with them much better than Arina had.

The baladi slowed, drums thumping a soft heartbeat. The dancers on stage flung their arms up and swayed into the last notes. When they finished, the audience clapped and trilled, and Arina patted her paws together and cheered with her tongue against the roof of her mouth, as loud as she could manage. Maybe, loudest of all.

The other acts were all familiar. The local dance community had brought out their best routines in honor of Siradi, but Arina had seen most of them at the most recent hafla. The pallas cat who owned the studio where the girls had taken lessons did her solo routine to a sharp, Egyptian tune. Her long silver fur rippled in sync with her purple costume, a tight dress with shapes cut out of it to allow her pelt to show. A trio of deer with zills performed a rapid, shimmy heavy, dance punctuated by the tapping of their hooves in time to the *ting-ting* of the finger cymbals.

By the time it was Siradi's turn, Arina had settled back in her seat, truly enjoying the dances, the music, and the sense of peace that had settled over her since her troupe's performance. Feeling bad for the ermine had somehow made it difficult to feel bad for herself. In fact, she felt a tickle of excitement as the lights dimmed and the curtain closed again for the first time since opening.

It was a clear signal of the main event, and the crowd fell

silent, hushed by the weight of that gesture, the velvet fabric, and the sense that something significant was about to happen.

Siradi. Arina's pulse quickened. She'd loved the honey badger ever since seeing her poster at the very first hafla she'd attended. Something about the way the dancer posed, so confident and fierce, had kindled Arina's urge to dance into a full-on fire. When she looked at Siradi, sparkling in her sequined belt and bra, Arina had known it for the first time—she *had* to dance.

Behind the curtain, the piper began with a single, wailing note. It stopped abruptly, a pause like a held breath, and then the stage exploded with sound. The curtain drew back in a rapid sweep, and the musicians flew into a song with more speed and fury than any of the previous acts. The rhythm was alien to Arina, far removed from her troupe's preferred baladi. The drums ran like a stampede, and the pipes twittered.

The coyote stepped forward, banging his drum between his paws. He lifted it over his head and signaled with it to the crowd, *pat, pat, pat.* The front rows began to clap in time to the beat. Offstage, a high-pitched trilling began. The clapping spread backward through the audience. Arina picked it up, despite the hafla tradition that applause was given with a trill. The coyote was clearly encouraging it, grinning and wagging his tail while the theater swelled with the beating of paws and drums and all at a pace that made Arina feel light-headed.

The excitement building in her belly, she clapped and watched the stage, as captive as the rest of them, waiting, waiting.

Siradi entered in full spin. She burst in from the right side of the stage, a blur of colored silk and sparkles. The trilling sounded again, as if all the other dancers huddled just out of range behind the curtain, and for that second only, Arina wished she were still among them.

The honey badger wore a ragged skirt of many layers, all

sheer and all in various shades of blue. She twirled a huge veil over her head as if she held a piece of the sky, and her bra and belt were crusted with silvery sequins.

Arina felt her chest tightening, realized she held her breath, that she clung to the back of the possum's chair with two tight fists. She forced her paws to release it and breathed, but remained forward and leaning, as if she could see better, hear better for the few inches difference.

Siradi stamped across the stage in time to the doumbeks. She bounced, jumping in place and spinning as she landed. The veil spun and folded in her hands as if by magic. She wrapped it around her flat head and somehow managed to peek through a slit that miraculously appeared. She grinned, bounced, and thrust her hips to one side.

Up, down, spin and bounce. The honey badger's routine was like nothing Arina had ever seen before. She barely undulated, focusing instead on accents and isolated lifts, drops, and jerking sideways movements. Her stout body left the ground completely every few steps, landing with a thundering impact that only made the crowd clap louder.

Siradi danced like a mad thing, using her bulk to her advantage, accentuating it, and the entire time grinning like she'd never had more fun in her life. She bounced, and stamped, and winked at any audience members she made eye contact with.

The clapping nearly drowned out the musicians. A few animals in the crowd stamped their paws against the floor until Arina lost the rhythm entirely. She had to assume Siradi could still hear the drums, though. The honey badger danced in a wild, careless fashion, so different from what Arina had learned, and yet, so exciting.

The crowd loved it. The other dancers loved it. Arina blinked back a film of tears and felt the truth of it in her bones. She loved it too. She loved to dance. If anyone could prove that to her, of course, it would be Siradi.

"It's the Turkish style." She lay on the banks of the river and watched Mella paddle in a circle. "Cabaret, it says on her website."

"What's that mean?" The capybara splashed with her front paws, holding her chin as high as she could manage in an attempt to tread water.

"It's faster and more energetic," Arina quoted from her weekend of online research. "The Turkish style is bouncier and less precise, but more celebratory."

She liked the idea of bouncy. She liked the way Siradi danced, even if she hadn't gotten a chance to actually meet her idol. At least she hadn't had to face Jayla either. The otter family had shuffled out the back after the performance along with the rest of the spectators. Non-dancers were not allowed backstage.

"Sounds like fun." Mella squinted at her.

"I'm just curious," Arina said. "I'd never seen it before."

"It would suit you."

"I'm not cut out for dancing."

"Sure."

The river sparkled and flowed past the capybara paddling about in its middle. The early afternoon sunlight made gems of the droplets encrusting Mella's hair. *Like sequins.* Arina watched them flash for a moment. *The Turkish costume is heavily sequined.*

"You *are* cut out for swimming," Mella called. "So, what are you doing on the bank all day?"

"Getting ready to swim circles around you." Arina grinned and dove into the river. She held her arms close to her sides, feet back and tail driving her forward like a furry bullet.

The dive took her to the sandy bottom, and she skimmed over it, enjoying the chill flowing through her pelt, the way the water made her lighter and at the same time pressed in from all sides. At the far bank, Arina flicked her paws and angled upward until she burst through the surface with a playful splash.

She sucked in a warm breath and then dove again, using her tail to propel her to the middle and then sweeping a graceful circuit around her friend. Then she surfaced, rolled onto her back, and floated in the current. A soft undulation of her tail kept her in place while the river parted around her, flowing past and away.

The sun warmed her belly, and the music of the water played a happy tune, one that lulled her thoughts sleepily back toward dancing. She imagined a costume sequined like a fish, a routine that leapt like the trout during the spring spawning.

Frantic splashing dragged her back to the moment. She rolled over lazily, expecting mischief on Mella's part. But when Arina scanned the river, she found no sign of the capybara.

"Mella?"

The river sparkled. The banks shone bright and green and empty.

"Mella!" Arina stuck her head underwater and caught a blur of brown fur to her right. She dove under just as the capybara breached the surface again. Instead of resuming her customary paddling, however, Mella pulled all four of her feet tight to her body, wiggled her butt, and sank like a rotund stone. She was too buoyant to reach the bottom, however, and bobbed halfway between surface and sand, writhing and twirling and not making a lick of headway.

Still, her paws remained glued to her sides. The capybara's cheeks puffed more than usual, and her eyes bugged under the strain of holding her breath. She gyrated, managed to end up head down, and then rolled over without making so much as an inch toward the surface.

Arina swam for her friend, shooting under her and

grabbing her around the middle. She dragged Mella to the surface, and the square head came up sputtering. They floated together with Mella resting against Arina's chest, and the otter's tail slowly working them toward the bank. When they reached it, she helped the capybara climb to safety before lunging out to lay panting in the grass.

Once she'd caught her breath, she sat up. "What happened?"

"Nothing." Mella gasped between pants. Her head hung so low her whiskers trailed through the grass.

"You weren't drowning?"

"No... Well, not exactly." The capybara blinked and fidgeted, combing the grass with her stout claws. "I was just trying something."

"Trying?" Arina stared at her friend as if she'd just grown a third pair of limbs. "What were you trying?"

Mella heaved a sigh and looked up and then immediately away. "I was trying to swim like you. Like an otter."

"You're not an otter."

"I know that." Mella shrugged stout shoulders and twitched her ears back. "It's just, you're so graceful in the water and I swim like a cork."

"But you don't have a tail." Arina checked just to be sure. Whatever appendage Mella might or might not have, it wasn't long enough even to require a tail hole in her swimsuit. "If you don't use your paws, you'll sink."

"I worked that out, Arina." Mella snorted. "Or didn't you notice?"

"Sorry." The otter squinted up at the sun. Her heart had stopped racing, now that Mella was not in danger of drowning. Her muscles unclenched, and she found a giggle bubbling in her chest. Trying to stifle it with both paws over her muzzle, she blinked away the last few water droplets.

"What?" Mella glared at her, suspicious and also, with a note in her voice that said she'd found the situation at least a little amusing as well.

"You." The giggle worked free. Arina hugged her arms to her sides and shook her head. "Trying to swim like an otter."

Mella grunted and climbed to her feet. She wiggled her butt and shrugged again. "I guess I can't be an otter, but I swim pretty good as a capybara."

"You do." Arina nodded. She eyed the river's surface, glittering like a thousand and one sequins. "And you know what? I can't dance like a weasel."

"What do you mean?" Mella stopped wagging her imaginary otter tail and stared.

"I think I dance pretty good as an otter, too."

"So do I," Mella said. "Does that mean you're cut out for bellydance after all?"

"Maybe." But Arina already scrambled to her feet. Her heart already heard a doumbek beating, faster, bouncier than the baladi. She saw sequins in her mind's eye, many layers of chiffon. "I've gotta go."

"Go." Mella grinned and waved her off. "Get to it, then."

The capybara's laughter followed Arina home, and though her heart still clutched at a shadow of fear, her feet moved fast and full of promise, each step a new idea and each breath a release as if something tight inside her slowly unwound back into place. She leapt through the fringe of trees along the river, dashed across the strip of meadow, and ran all the way home.

The doumbeks pounded at the rear of the stage. A pipe wailed, and the beat she'd been practicing to for weeks began. Beyond the stage, the hafla crowd trilled and stamped. Her parents were there, along with Mella, who'd patiently watched and commented on rehearsal after rehearsal while Arina worked on her choreography. On the far side of the planks, her old troupe waited with the other dancers.

She smiled, and though Jayla dropped her gaze quickly

away, the other girls grinned back. Arina closed her eyes and breathed. She listened to the trills of her friends and family. She listened to the drums and the pipes, and she let the music seep into her, filling her body until her muscles had no choice but to move. She swayed as the music built. She lifted her veil and bent her knees, bouncing in place and waiting for the note that would cue her entrance.

Her skirts flowed like the river water. Her belt and bra shimmered like silver fish, like sunlight on the current. Arina rolled her paws as if she were swimming and flowed with the music out onto the stage. She stamped, and the stage trembled. She bounced, and the crowd began to clap. Arnina danced like an otter. She played, and she hopped, and she wiggled through the routine with the doumbeks punctuating each movement, and the pipes sounding a lot like water flowing.

She danced, because it was inside her. She danced alone, so that the only thing she might tower over was her own shadow and the only thing she had to worry about was listening, moving, and letting go. Her heart lifted with the beat, fluttering as the pipe warbled. Arina closed her eyes and moved for herself only.

She was made for dancing.

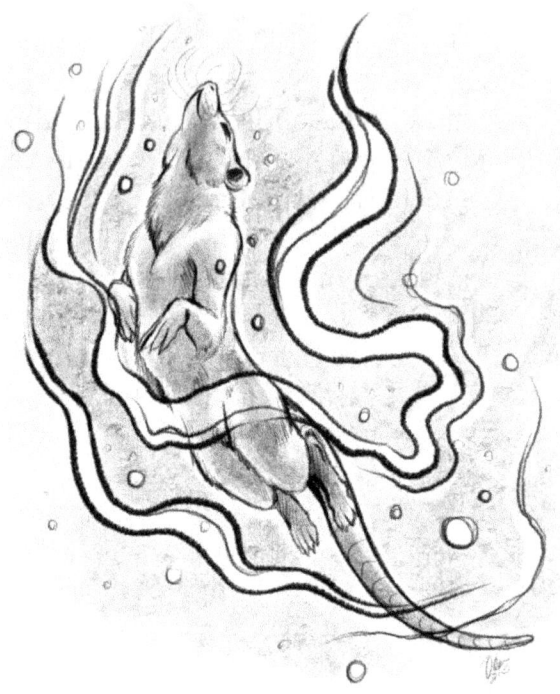

TJ Minde

TJ is a rat – I mean otter, totally an otter; sleek fur, love for feesh and all of that – that moved to Ohio almost ten years ago. After scurrying – I mean diving, then swimming like otter do – into the fandom, he picked up the pen. TJ is incredible grateful for the community of artists, writers and friend he found; they helped him discover something that he cares about – writing. TJ enjoys squeaking – and chirping! Can't forget that – with others about the worlds and characters they've created.

TJ's other stories may be found in issues of FANG, Heat and other anthologies both in and out of the fandom. For thoughts, comments and replies in bite-sized chunks, he can be found on Twitter @TJMinde.

Do you think he's otter-ly adorable?

RIVERS

The giant otter paced back and forth in the living room, picking at the sleeves of his shirt. His paws moved from his wrists to the stylish vest his girlfriend made him squeeze into every time they went out together. With a sigh, he sunk into the plush couch in the living room. He lolled his head over the back of the couch, wishing he wasn't going dancing that night. *I hope it's worth it,* he thought.

The sound of shoes clacking on the hardwood floors drew his attention to the hallway.

"Okay, Michael, let's go." The smaller river otter walked in with a paw to her ear, fiddling with a silver earring. She stood about a head shorter than him at full height. Her black dress clung to her chest, flowing down her small form with bold silver lines accenting its edges.

It took Michael a moment to process the words she had said. "God, you look great."

Her lip curled in a knowing smile. "Of course I do. Now, get off your ass and let's go." She turned away from him and was halfway out the door before he understood what she had said.

We look great together, he thought as he chased after her.

Michael shifted his car into park. Janet kept clicking away at her phone. "We're here." He pulled the emergency brake out of habit.

"I know, one second," she said with a wave of her paw. The small otter held her phone up, pouted, and snapped a selfie. Without a word to him, she stared at the device, altering the picture until it was just right. "And posted." She dropped her cell into a matching purse she kept around her wrist. "Now I'm ready."

Before the giant otter could respond, Janet opened the door and stepped out into the night, leaving Michael to scramble after her.

The chatter of people and a thumping beat cut through the evening. While there was no line outside the two-story building, the open balcony that wrapped around the upper floor was packed as usual. Just over the door was a fluorescent sign that read "Cool's" with a stylized wave under it and blue musical notes all around. Quarter and eighth notes danced around the front under the balcony, bordering it.

"Pay him," said the river otter, nodding to the bouncer.

Michael pulled out his wallet. "Yes, dear."

The bear at the door checked their IDs and took Michael's cash without a word, and in they went. The din of conversation flowed as people of every shape, size, and gender sat at tables laid about the space. Others gathered at the bar lined with beer taps and bottles of wine along the wall.

"Want a drink?" Michael asked.

She rolled her eyes. "You know I don't drink down here. Come on." She led him to the other side of the club where the conversations were drowned out by the music coming from the stairwell.

He looked longingly at the line of beer taps. *She knows I prefer the ones here.* Nevertheless, he followed Janet's lead.

While the first floor had a calm atmosphere, the second was jumping. Loud dance music drowned out the thoughts in Michael's head while bright lights flashed and spun around the room. Bodies, packed wall to wall, moved to the beat of the music.

Janet leaned close to the giant otter and pulled him down by his collar. "Cranberry and vodka," she said into his ear and nodded to the one wall that didn't give access outside. Before he could respond, the river otter slipped away with her tail bouncing to the beat.

With a sigh, Michael did as he was told. The giant otter wasn't able to swim through the crowds like Janet could. His size didn't afford him the same graceful motions. So with constant apologies, Michael bumped into people as he made his way past gyrating bodies and worked towards a colorful wall.

Light from behind the bar shined like a rainbow. Bottles of varying shape, size, and color filled the back wall. Gin, vodka, tequila, rum. Nothing he liked.

Unlike downstairs, very few folks just stood around. The ones that were there got their drinks and shimmied back to the dance floor. It didn't take Michael long to catch the bartender's eye.

"What ya want?" she shouted over the thumping bass.

Setting his paws on the edge of the surface, the otter leaned closer. "Cranberry and vodka." She nodded her head without a word, she stepped back to make the drink.

He rose back to full height and watched as the woman behind the counter flowed from bottle to bottle, moving around with even motions. She was in her element, sure and steady in what she was doing. *Man...I wish I had that kind of confidence.* His gaze fell to the bar. *My friends usually have to pull it out of me.*

A short glass filled with a ruby liquid slid in to Michael's view. When he looked up, the bartender waited there expectantly. Without a word between them, he fished his card from his wallet.

"Just the one?" she asked. Michael nodded, handing her his card. "Tab?"

The large otter shook his head and the bartender processed the payment. Once it was returned, Michael took the glass and fought his way through the crowd again. The loud music drummed in his ears as people around him danced and bounced to the beat.

The otter stared at the grinning muzzles around him. *It's so loud; how do people find this fun?* Step by step, he made his way back to where he saw Janet move into the crowd and attempted to follow her. Pushing his way into the writhing, dancing mass of people, Michael held the glass high, ensuring no stray elbows or swinging paw spilled the contents.

Moving deeper into the tightly packed crowds, the giant otter scanned the dancers for his girlfriend. Mammals of every shape, size, and type moved and spun around him, each with their own scent, further confusing him. *Not her. Not them,* Michael chanted as he looked from person to person.

He finally caught sight of her silver earrings shining in the bright neon lights of the club. By the way she moved, anyone could see she was in her element; the beat was her current, and boy could she swim.

Michael cut past the couples and groups in motion, making his way to her.

The giant otter leaned in close and held the drink out to her. "Here you are, Janet."

She opened half an eye and located the mixture. Her paw floated toward it, still moving with the beat, and pulled it from Michael's. As she sipped from the glass, Janet closed her eye again. All the while, her hips and shoulders swung to the music. And as the cocktail was lowered, it too became a part of her motion, like another extension of her body.

For a moment, Michael stood there. The music hammered at him again and again. Everyone around him moved and swayed with the rhythm. *Well, I wanted to be here with her. Might as well try to have fun with it. When in Rome, right?*

The otter picked up the steady 1-2-3-4 drumming against his body and dipped a shoulder to the rhythm. A breath later, be began swaying his hips from side to side. He shuffled closer to Janet, trying to dance with her. *God, I probably stick out like a sore thumb.* Still moving, he took a breath, compelling himself to relax as his ears warmed in a blush.

Michael forced a smile on his face as he opened his eyes and tried to ignore his feelings by focusing on the beauty in front of him. Janet's swaying hips, her flowing arms, her sexy confidence. As he watched her move, his smile grew genuine. *This really is her element. She's having so much fun. Maybe I can, too.*

The river otter took another sip of her drink and opened her eyes. She stared at the giant otter and his awkward movements for a beat before spinning around in a smooth circle and eased her way back into the crowd and away from Michael.

The smile fell from the giant otter's muzzle. His ears followed suit, sinking low, and he thought as his shoulders slumped. He stopped trying to dance and instead made more apologies as he worked his way through the crowd. *This really isn't my scene. I'd much rather be rolling dice with my friends...*

He sighed a silent sigh drowned out by the music and flopped on to a padded bench resting against the wall. Michael scanned the crowd, watching as people danced. The pounding bass grew louder causing his head to throb. Splaying his ears against his head, the giant otter pressed a paw to the bridge of his muzzle. *Maybe I'll just grab a drink from downstairs.*

"You okay?"

Michael jumped as a woman spoke into his ear.

"I'm sorry," she quickly added, setting a paw on his shoulder. "I didn't mean to scare you."

The giant otter looked up at her. She was a marine otter, with a dark brown paw balled into a fist against her chest and worry in her black eyes. She wore a plaid skirt and a dark band tee.

Michael took a breath and shook his head. He leaned in,

already up to her chin. "No need to apologize. Just didn't hear you. Wasn't expecting it."

She nodded. "Well, you looked dejected, and I wanted to see if you were interested in dancing with me?"

He smiled and shook his head again. "Thanks for the offer, but this isn't really my crowd."

The marine otter tilted her head in confusion before looking from the bench to him. Michael read the silent question and slid over, offering her a seat.

"If this isn't your crowd, why are you here?" she asked.

Michael shrugged. "This is my girlfriend's river, not mine."

She looked at him with a raised eyebrow. "What's that supposed to mean?"

The giant otter gave a half-smile. "Oh, it's something my family says. This is where she belongs; I don't swim here."

"Oh. And where's she?" asked the woman in the band tee. Michael simply nodded to the sea of people. "Why aren't you with her? Or she with you?"

Again, the giant otter shrugged. "As I said: this is her river. She likes to dance, and I don't. Besides, she's told me before that I move worse than a drunken elephant with a lampshade on his head." He forced a laugh.

The marine otter scanned the crowd. "Which one's her?"

He looked around the room again in earnest. It took him a moment, but he found Janet and pointed her out. "Black dress, silver lines, dancing with a fox."

She looked in the direction he pointed. The fox stood behind his girlfriend with his black paws on her waist, grinding his pelvis against her rear. Janet wiggled her hips in kind to the beat as she wrapped her arms around the fox's neck.

The marine otter stared. "That's not dancing, that's foreplay."

Michael shrugged. "She's just letting loose. No big deal."

"If you say so. She's your girlfriend, not mine," she said with a shrug. "If this isn't your river, want to grab a beer instead?" She pointed over her shoulder towards the stairs. The marine otter jumped up and watched in awe as Michael stood. Unsurprisingly, the giant otter towered over her by two heads. "Dude, you're huge."

Michael barely heard her, but the sentiment was not new. He was always the tall beacon that everyone looked for. He was hard to miss.

The two made their way to the first floor and, when the music dulled to a background thumping, he sighed in relief.

"Nice to hear your own thoughts again, right?" said the marine otter behind him.

Michael nodded. "Yeah. I can do some loud music, but that's just too much."

She nodded. "I can understand that. It may not be for everyone. But, if it isn't for you, why do you come?"

He shrugged. "As I said, she wants to dance, so I take her."

The smaller woman chuckled. "I got that. But, why do you still come? Can't she come dance on her own while you do something else *you* enjoy?"

He didn't answer her right away. Instead, he worked his way to the lower bar. Once he had the older wolf's attention, he handed him his card. "Draft pilsner and whatever she'd like." He gestured to the marine otter close behind him.

"Oh, uh. Do you have an IPA you'd recommend?"

Without a word, the bartender nodded and stepped away.

"This is the first time I've bought someone a drink without even catching their name first." He held out a paw. "I'm Michael."

"Donna. And, thanks for the drink." Her brown paw disappeared into his gray one. "So, let's try this again." She smiled. "If clubs aren't your thing, and you aren't there with your girlfriend"—she pointed upstairs—"why *are* you here?"

"Here you go," said the wolf, placing both glasses on the

bar. "Tab?"

Saved by the wolf. Michael looked from the wolf to Donna. She shrugged. "Why not. I may have another anyway."

With a flick of his ear, the bartender walked off.

"Let's grab a seat." As he walked past Donna, a half smirk crossed the smaller otter's muzzle.

"You know I'm just gonna ask the question again, right?" she called behind him, amusement bright in her voice.

Michael ignored the comment. "So, how'd you find this place?" He set his glass down on the far end of the bar and took a seat.

Donna shook her head as she sat beside him. "Some friends of mine knew some folks that used to play back there." She nodded to the currently unused stage. "We've come here a few times since and just enjoyed ourselves. With or without them. But, tonight, I'm here alone. You?" She sipped her beer.

The giant otter nodded. "I've been coming here for years. Janet and I had friends in high school that came by all the time. They'd dance or watch the live bands. It was one of the few places we could be treated almost like adults before we were. Taught us how to behave before it really mattered."

"Is that why you keep coming back? Nostalgia?"

He started into his beer, thinking for another moment. "Maybe? I mean, I like hanging out down here. When there's a live band, the place comes alive in a different way."

Donna nodded with him. "So it's just upstairs that you don't swim in."

The giant otter grinned. "Yeah. The music up there is rarely to my taste. Neither is the way folks dance these days."

"That still doesn't quite answer why you come."

She's not gonna let me out easy, is she? Michael sipped his drink again. "Well, I guess it's that I want to spend time with Janet."

"Your girlfriend?" She asked. Michael nodded in reply. "But, she doesn't want to spend time with you?"

Michael turned to her. "I wouldn't say that. Sometimes she wants a designated driver."

"So she uses you?"

"No, no," Michael said immediately. "We're a couple. There's...other stuff we do." He paused and cleared his throat. "*Couple things.*" He watched to see if she caught on.

"You have sex."

Michael shrunk in his chair. "I mean, I wasn't going to say that, but yeah. And, I haven't heard her complain yet."

Donna shook her head. "Don't know why sex is so shameful for men."

"Hey, we just met."

The marine otter shrugged. "It's a standard function of people. You do it, I do it. The bartender does it. Par for the course." She sipped the hoppy beer again. "So, what is it you like to do? Yourself, I mean. Not the sex bits. Where *is* your river?"

With a blush in his ears, Michael rose up in his bar stool. "I like tabletop games."

"Really? Pen and paper, or board?"

The giant otter's eyes shined. "Both. You play?"

Donna shook her head. "I'd like to dip my toe in that pool one day, but I don't do much yet. My friends want to get me into it, though."

"Well, I really hope you get the chance. Is there any—"

A paw brushed along his back and someone cleared their throat. Michael looked over his shoulder and there was Janet. "Oh, hi honey. I was just talking with my new friend, Donna."

She didn't acknowledge the other woman. "I'm going to go club hopping with a new friend. You can go home if you want. And, don't feel like you have to wait up for me." Before the giant otter could respond, Janet turned away.

"Yes dear," he called after her. "Goodnight." He watched as

she walked towards the front door and walked out with the fox that had been grinding against her.

"Is that normal?" Donna asked.

He shook his head. "Not always, but she's done it once or twice. She usually drags me from place to place. It's kinda nice to not have to go for once."

"Do you know that fox she was with?"

"Nope." Michael sipped his beer. "But she hasn't introduced me to her friends and hasn't had much of an interest in meeting mine."

This time, it was Donna's turn to stare into her glass. "Well, that's unfortunate."

Michael rose to his feet. "I think I'm gonna cash out and head home then."

"What? Wait, why?" she reached a paw out to his arm. "Just because she told you to?" The giant otter looked back and read the confusion and something else in her eye.

The giant otter shrugged. "Why not?"

"Because you're your own person?" Her shoulders fell as she broke eye contact. "And, I'm enjoying our conversation."

Did I hurt her feelings? Man, have I really gotten that out of touch with people? Where's the real-life perception check?

After a breath, Donna continued. "Maybe we can have another drink and talk some more?" Donna looked back quickly, raised her paws. "Not looking for anything else. Just a friend to talk with."

Michael sat back down. "Shouldn't that be my line as the guy here?"

"Hey, chicks can be thirsty too." She winked. "But, really, I'm just looking for the company. Why not tell me about some of the games you've played or the character's you've built."

The giant otter stared at Donna. "Sounds like you know more about tabletop games than you let on."

"Just because I don't play doesn't mean I haven't done my

research." The marine otter winked.

"Fine, fine, you talked me into it. Let me get another beer first."

The two talked for hours like old friends about board and tabletop games. Then, they talked about video games, which transitioned to comics and movies before they eventually looped back around to music.

As he finished his final glass of water, Michael smiled at the other otter. "I really have to thank you. I don't think I've had this much fun at Cool's in a while. At least not without a band playing."

"And I'm really glad you stayed. You're a really fun guy, Michael." Donna punched him on the shoulder.

The giant otter grinned. "Hey, I'm not a mushroom."

Donna rolled her eyes with a smile. "Ugh. Are we at the pun-stage of our friendship?"

"Nope. That's just what happens when you get me talking. Punning isn't a stage, it's a way of life." He scribbled his signature across the check and slid it back across the bar. "If you don't pun, *water* you waiting for?" He side her glass closer to her. "Though, if they aren't your thing, you *otter* stop me before I really get going. Otherwise, you'll have to swim through my sea of puns."

Donna set her paws over her ears. "Stop, stop! It hurts!" She grinned all the while.

Michael crossed his arms. "Only because you asked so nicely." He checked his watch. "I really should get going."

The marine otter stood from her seat. "Yeah, me too. Thank you for keeping me company."

Holding out a paw, Michael shook his head. "No, you saved me from a boring night alone. I should be thanking you. I hope we'll run into each other again."

Again, Donna's small paw disappeared in the giant otter's.

"I hope so too. Maybe we can reach the 'trade numbers' stage of the friendship then."

"That would be nice." He patted himself down. "Phone, wallet, keys. I think I'm good. May I walk you to your car?" Michael held out an arm.

"If I didn't know any better, I'd think you're flirting with me." The marine otter giggle taking the offered arm.

Michael jumped. "Wait, I'm not—I mean, I hope I don't come off as flirtatious. I'm just trying to be polite."

Donna squeezed his arm. "Chill out, Michael. You're being a total gentleman. I'm playing around." She stepped forward, sliding her arm from his and walked.

It took the giant otter a breath to realize she was heading to the door. In two large steps, he caught up to her. He walked her out of Cool's, then to her car. Once she drove off, he got into his vehicle and did the same.

Michael made his way up the walk humming a tune and slid his key into the door. *I haven't felt this good in a while.*

Inside, the lights were on inside and Janet sat on the couch. A half full wine glass sat beside what looked to be an empty bottle.

"Finally, you're home," said the river otter, jumping up from the couch. She looked like she was about to run to Michael, but stumbled her way to him and fell into his arms.

The giant otter rubbed the back of her head. "How much have you had to drink tonight?"

"Not much. One or two at the other clubs we went to, and the bottle of wine I had waiting for you, but that's not important." Wrapping her paws behind his neck, Janet stood on her tip toes and pulled him down, kissing him passionately on the lips.

Michael pushed her away. "What's gotten into you?"

"Nothing, and that's the problem," Janet said with a

flirtatious smile. She began running her paws over the giant otter's body. "I worked myself up dancing, and now I want the real thing—not to be teased."

"Honey." He pushed back against her. "You know I don't like it this way."

Janet kissed at his neck. "Oh, come on. It's always your way. Why don't I get what I want?"

Michael rolled his eyes. "Dammit, Janet."

She finally took a step back. "What Michael? I want to get laid. You gonna call me a slut next or take me to the bedroom?"

The giant otter didn't respond and instead pushed past her.

"Didja change your mind?" Janet asked.

He stopped with his paw on the dresser drawer. "No. I was just going to change. Then I'm going to sleep on the couch tonight." He grabbed his sleeping clothes and walked toward the bathroom.

"Michael wait," she said.

The giant otter didn't meet her gaze. "We can talk in the morning when you're sober." He closed the door behind him. A moment later, the bedroom door slammed shut.

Michael had trouble falling asleep. Instead, his mind kept wandering back to that evening. Back to Donna and their talk. He thought about how easily they spoke about games and about the guys he made those memories with. His friends that Janet only met for a moment and had no interest meeting again. He thought about how stilted things have been with him and Janet. About how tough it was to talk with her.

The giant otter thought about how easy it was for Janet to flow at the club, but she always swam alone—or with someone else she met there.

She never swam with him. He thought about how much he wanted someone to swim with.

Michael had no idea how long he laid there, but he finally

fell asleep.

The following morning was quiet. He tiptoed around the house, letting the river otter sleep as much as she wanted. He made coffee, rice and was frying up two eggs when she finally stirred.

"I hope you're satisfied," she said as he grabbed a mug and poured coffee.

"With what?"

She served herself rice and took the two eggs Michael was making. "I hope you liked sleeping alone last night and not getting laid."

He cracked two more eggs into the frying pan and shrugged. "Sleeping alone wasn't the worst thing last night. In some senses, it was kinda nice."

"'Nice?' The hell you mean, 'nice?'"

Michael shrugged again. "It gave me time to think about things. About what's important."

"Michael, what the hell are you talking about?"

He stared at the eggs in the pan for a moment. "I'm not happy, Janet. We do so much out of obligation. I take you places you want to go, but you never return the favor. You know where you fit in, and you've tried to make me fit into the mold of who you wanted me to be, not who I am."

Janet crossed her arms. "And where are you going with this?"

The giant otter slid his eggs on top of a second dish of rice. "I want to find out where I fit in. I want to find my river, where I know how to move and act. I want someone who can swim with me." He stared at the dish of food for a breath. "I think we should see other people."

The river otter sat there in silence for a moment. "Your loss." Without another word, she picked up her bowl and returned to the bedroom.

Michael called Jack and asked for a place to crash for a few nights. The ferret let him. There were no questions or comments. Just a couch with his legs hanging off the end, a pillow and blanket. It wasn't the best night sleep, but it was better than nothing.

The giant otter spent the rest of the day moping on the couch. He had been with Janet longer than he'd been without her. And, being on his own again was scary. His friend let him be for the most part. The ferret brought him a proper breakfast and lunch, but did not force conversation on him. Later the next afternoon Michael made his way to Janet's home for some essentials.

After a shower and a fresh outfit, he almost began to feel better.

"Want anything special for dinner?" Jack asked.

Michael shook his head.

The ferret nodded. "Okay then. Anything you don't want?"

Again, the giant otter shook his head.

"Great." Jack smiled and grabbed his keys. "Then we're having an emergency game night."

"I don't know if I really want to see everyone else yet," protested the otter. "Besides, I don't have any of my stuff."

Jack clapped him on the shoulder. "That's fine. You won't need it." He then typed out a quick message on his phone. "Okay, the table knows. I'll be sure you have fun."

"I don't know, Jack." Still, Michael let himself be led to the car.

The two stopped at a fast-casual burrito place before the ferret pushed Michael back into the car.

"Dude, where're we going?" he finally asked.

Jack smiled. "I told you, to a place where you won't need your things. Just sit back and relax."

With a sigh, the giant otter did as he was told. Scrunched up in the ferret's car, he closed his eyes. The vehicle swayed this way and that as Jack drove on. Michael's mind wandered to past trips to Cool's—to the others Janet danced with.

"She'll have more fun without me anyway," he muttered.

Jack set a comforting paw on the otter's leg. "Hey, don't worry about her. We'll all help you through this." The ferret was talking about the others at the table.

Michael just nodded. A second later, Jack engaged the brake and patted Michael's leg, getting his attention.

"We're here," he said with a smile.

The otter fought his way out of the vehicle and looked to the building. The words "Dice Tavern" were surrounded by a full set of polyhedral dice. "What's this place?" he asked.

"A new gaming bar. Now, let's grab a beer. The others are already inside." The ferret led them in.

As they entered the building, a cheer went up from a table and pint glasses were raised. "Jeez, you guys," Michael said as he saw his friends greeting him with open arms.

"I'm so glad to be back at the table." Michael grinned. "What are we playing?"

"I've got a new adventure for us," Jack said. "A simple homebrew to play around with and be silly; everyone's a bard."

The entire table stared at him for a moment. Then, Michael chuckled. Followed by another. Before too long, the whole table fell into a giggling fit.

"Wow." Michael shook his head. "This will certainly be something. Let me grab a drink first."

The giant otter approached the bar. The list of draft craft beers was long. *Jack really knows the right place to cheer me up.*

He looked for the bartender and saw her slide a tall glass to another otter and took her payment. *No way?*

Michael smiled and walked up beside the shorter otter. "Fancy meeting you twice in one weekend."

Donna turned to him and smiled. "Michael? No way. I

thought I'd run into you at Cool's next."

The giant otter nodded. "I was thinking the same. You here with friends?"

She shook her head. "Nah. Wanted to see what they had to play. Didn't think I'd end up staying long. You?"

"Yup. Our DM, Jack, has some sort of one-shot planned tonight."

"What's that?"

"Hmm?" He flicked an ear in confusion before his own words clicked in his head. "Oh, sorry about the jargon."

Donna shook her head. "Don't worry about it. You said this was your river. Enjoy the swim."

A goofy grin crossed his muzzle and his ears lowered. "It's a game that is meant to be played in one session. We may never use these characters again, but hopefully we'll have a few interesting stories to tell."

"And Janet is okay with you being here."

Michael's gaze fell and he stared at the bar. "We...broke up."

"I'm sorry." She set a paw on the giant otter's arm. "Anything I can do to help?"

Michael shrugged. "I'll get over it on my own. Oh, hey, you said you wanted to play a pen a paper RPG; care to join us?"

"I'd like that. But would your friends mind a stranger joining you?" She smiled at him.

The giant otter waved her off. "It wouldn't be the first time someone brought a newbie to the table. I'll help you, even."

"Well then, it sounds like a plan."

Michael ordered a beer, then, with Donna beside him, they walked back to the table. "Hey guys, this is Donna. I met her at Cool's yesterday. Is it alright if she joins us tonight?" he asked the group.

All of them shook their heads.

"We're playing with pre-generated characters, so it's no problem," Jack said, handing pages out. "Here's two."

Michael slid a page to the marine otter and then took his time introducing her to the others at the table while Jack set up the session.

"Okay." The ferret clapped his paws together. "Let's begin. Like any good adventure, you start in a tavern. There's a band on stage playing a bawdy tune."

Michael grinned. "In that case, care to dance?" he said to Donna.

"Thought you'd never ask," she answered.

Jack smiled. "Roll the profession check; let's see how well you do."

Anastasia Spinet

Anastasia Spinet is a spider lady who lives in a rather watery corner of Southern New England where she spends much of her time observing the native wildlife (including the incredibly adorable river otters) and using their antics as inspiration for her stories. She shares her home with an entourage of felines, a rat, and a Pomeranian. When not writing or nature watching, she's usually playing D&D or indulging in comically terrible films.

WHERE DEAD THINGS SLUMBER

"I had that dream again."

"Really, now?" Mae's scaled hands deftly worked her knitting needles. Her rocking chair squeaked beneath her as the large alligator rocked back and forth in her wooden seat. "Tell me again how it goes."

Mae was the only one in town who owned a heated lounging pool in her living room and, having no children of her own, frequently let Samuel use it in the winter months. After his sister disappeared into the white, the young otter was certain he hated winter even more than the gator did. She never said anything about it, but he was an observant kit, and he was certain she knew.

Sam let himself sink up to his round black nose, relishing the warmth of the water, before raising his head to answer her. "It starts the same as always, except it was snowing this time." He paused, considering that maybe it wasn't exactly the same as always. This was the first time it was snowing in the dream. There was always snow on the ground, but this was the first time it fell from the sky. "The woman was there."

"The one with the mask?" Click, click went Mae's needles.

Sam swallowed and nodded. "Yeah."

The masked woman was always the worst part of the dream. Her species was perpetually indeterminate – sometimes she looked like a fox, sometimes like a wolf, other times like a stag. But she always had a mask, perfectly round and carved of bleached bone, featureless but for two round eyeholes filled with the blackness of the void. A straight red line ran from the base of the right eye down to her chin, as if she had cried a single tear of blood.

"The two lights were on her shoulders again, and a third in her one hand, but the other was empty like before."

"She hold it out to you?" The rocking chair protested beneath the gator woman's girth. Contained within its hearth, the fire crackled merrily, its golden light dancing along her green-grey scales.

Sam could feel the water around him getting cold, the fire that fed its warmth dying outside in the chill of the winter storm. "Yeah," he said. "And, no, I didn't take it."

"Maybe you should one of these days." Mae set her knitting down on the polished table beside her and stood, smoothing her dark grey dress as she did so. Mae lived humbly and dressed plain, but, born of a large and wealthy family down south, her clothes and home were made of fine material, hinting at her hidden wealth.

"I can't, though!" Sam's intestines coiled at the thought, the blurry image of the ghostly woman's paws sinking into his mind, her dark gaze colder than the ice that incarcerated the old beaver pond far out in the woods. "I'm scared."

"All the more reason to take it. She might have something to tell you." Mae lumbered over to the door, her claws reaching for the heavy iron handle. "Want me to keep the fire going out there, hon?"

Sam glanced behind himself at the window overlooking the lounging pool. It was plastered in white snow.

"No," he said, standing and reaching for a towel hanging from a hook nailed to the wall behind him. "I'm alright. I should probably get going anyway."

"Any time, dear." She returned to her seat and her knitting. "You are always welcome here."

"I know," Sam said. Turning away, he toweled off his sleek brown and cream fur before pulling on his baggy winter pants and coat. He tied a red wool scarf, knitted for him by Mae herself, around his neck, tucking it up over his sensitive nose. "Thank you."

"Tell your mother I said hello."

Sam hoped she didn't see him flinch as he pulled on his scuffed leather boots. Beneath the sanctuary of his scarf, he pulled back his lips back from his fangs in a grimace of shame. His mother hadn't been the same since Kate disappeared. None of them had, but his mother had exceptionally transformed once the grief took hold and began to germinate. She insisted always that Sam was a bother to Mae, despite the gator's insistence to the contrary, and he anticipated a lecture each time Mother knew when he went to see her. Sam, however, knew the real reason for his mother's reluctance to let him visit – she was afraid for him each time he left the house.

"I will," he muttered, so used to lying about it at this point that he didn't even feel guilty anymore. Sam trudged to the door in his heavy black boots and thick coat, ready to brave the storm. "Have a good night, Mae."

"You too, hon." Click. Rock, creak.

Sam nodded and fingered the latch on the iron handle, pushing the door outward. The cold air momentarily swirled inside in a cyclone of bitterness, and then the young otter stepped forward into the blur of white.

The trees rose high into the pale sky like the arms of the dead, and the wind sang its shrill, keening song as it wound its way through their reaching fingers. Snow fell thick and heavy from weeping clouds, and a white shroud blanketed the land.

Sam stood chilled and alone amidst the storm, the flakes stinging his nose and crystalizing upon his dark whiskers. He drew his heavy buckskin coat around him, but it did little to keep out the cold; somehow the wind found its way beneath his leathery shield, brushing itself through his fur so deeply that it reached flesh and bone, chilling the otter to his core.

He ran aimlessly, losing himself in the woods. The trees looked like all the other trees surrounding his town, tall maples and towering oaks. Everything looked the same in all directions, nothing but whiteness and tall, grey sentinels.

Then he saw it through the haze, a single golden light, bobbing merrily between the trees. A lantern! Was it his father come to rescue him? Perhaps Mae? That was no matter. Relief washed over him, for he would no longer be so lost, so alone.

Sam ran towards the golden light, stumbling clumsily through the waist-high snow, his paw raised above his head in greeting.

"Hey!" he shouted, his voice muffled by the mantle of snow. "Over here!"

If an answer came, Sam could not hear it above the wind's howling, but in response to his call, the lantern grew brighter, its bearer drawing nearer amidst the storm.

Elated, a relieved grin spreading itself across his muzzle, Sam doubled his pace, nearly tripping once over a snow-covered log in his excitement. The cold bit deep beneath his clothes, his fur; he could not wait to be back in the warm safety of his bed or nestled before Mae's fireplace with a warm cup of hot cocoa cradled in his thawing paws.

He stopped short when he saw the shape that emerged from the veil. The red robes, the black eyes, the form that was hard to look at – shifting hazily from fox to coyote, from otter to stag. Sam's blood froze as still as the icicles descending from the branches above. It was not his father, nor mother, nor Mae come to save him.

It was *her.*

"No," Sam mouthed, his lips forming themselves around the word, but his throat too paralyzed by fear to make the sound. Not this dream again, not this nightmare. The otter willed himself to wake up, but his tired body, wherever it slept in the waking world, rebelled in indifferent silence.

The woman stared into him with her hollow eyes of judgement. She spread her willowy arms wide, her crimson and white robes somehow impervious to the violence of the storm's breath. Within her right paw appeared a bloom of golden light, followed by a second and third above her shoulders. She held her left paw open to him, beckoning.

Take it. Take it, said a voice in his head, though Sam didn't know who it belonged to, himself or the woman.

"*I can't, though!*" His own words came floating back to him, the memory fresh and clean. "*I'm too scared.*"

Naturally, this was followed by the memory of Mae and her wisdom: "*All the more reason to take it.*"

Terror held Sam's heart in its crushing grip, but the otter knew Mae was right. The woman had to tell him something, and he could only begin to understand it if he took her paw. But it scared him so much, her white mask and her nebulous, indeterminate form. He hated the uncertainty of her – Sam liked for things to be concrete and regular, such as how two plus two would always equal four or how the sky was always blue on a sunny day. He didn't like things like this woman; abstract things like fear and grief.

Sam, however, wanted to be free of her. He wanted her to go and never bother him again, and the otter knew, somewhere in the illogical portion of his soul, that in order to make her leave, he needed to understand.

Moving against the fear that held him in thrall, Sam reached out a dark, webbed paw and gently, oh so gently, touched the soft pads of his fingers to hers.

He woke with a blinding start, lurching bolt upright in bed, his chest heaving, his paw pads clammy with sweat. The otter was safe within his room, surrounded by the familiar wood-paneled walls and warm – if not overheated – beneath his plaid wool covers.

Again with that horrible nightmare. Worse, he'd done as

Mae had said, he'd taken the woman's paw, but he felt no closer to understanding her message (if there even was a message at all) than he had before. Bitter with anger, Sam smoothed a paw over his bristly whiskers before curling back into bed, pressing his face into a pillow that was still damp with tears.

Monday. Back to the middle school grind.

Sam shouldered his backpack, adjusting the too-thick straps around his too-thin body. Normally, he'd wait at the end of his street with Kate for the bus, but since she'd been gone, he'd gotten in the habit of walking. He didn't like the noise and commotion of the bus without her. The loneliness made him feel alien and unwelcome, a sullen, silent lump amidst a sea of happy, screaming kids.

He had grown to like the walk, even with the snow. Sometimes he'd imagine Kate was there, walking alongside him, and he'd be overwhelmed by a wistful sadness, wondering why they never did this together while she was here. She loved nature, and the path through the woods to school took him past all sorts of wonders that he knew would be lovely in the spring when they were flourishing with verdant blooms. Why hadn't they done this?

"Because you're a nerd!" said the not-Kate, the phantom Kate conjured by his mind who pranced alongside him, lovingly taunting him in her sing-song voice. "Because you're a nerd who just wants to stay in and do math all day."

"I'm not a nerd," Sam muttered under his breath, streams of foggy breath coiling out from behind his scarf. "I'm just practical."

"Practical schmactical." The not-Kate spun on her heel, her winter-inappropriate skirt billowing around her as she twirled. "You just don't have enough imagination. Go out and see the woods sometime."

Sam huffed, trudging along. His throat tightened and his

eyes prickled. He told himself it was the nonexistent wind.

"Big neeeeeerd!" The not-Kate puffed out her cheeks and waved her webbed paws at him, speaking in that teasing voice she always used when she wanted to make him laugh.

Even though it wasn't really Kate, her methods still worked; a short bark of laughter, choked with unshed tears, escaped Sam's muzzle. "Fine, I'll go into the woods for a bit." He stepped off the path, the underbrush shedding its snowy crust as he moved. "But not for too long. I can't be late."

"Chickenshit." Kate's phantom was beside of him now, whispering into his ears. "Be a man. Play hooky."

"No."

The sound of clucking behind him.

Sam smiled, imagining Kate tucking her balled paws beneath her armpits and flapping her elbows as if they were wings.

"No hooky," Sam said with finality. "I will, however, go deeper into the woods than I intended to. A compromise."

"Go to the beaver pond," suggested the not-Kate. "It's magical."

Sam rolled his chocolate brown eyes. "There is no such thing as magic."

"Says you." The phantom Kate stood in front of him again, sticking out her tongue.

Sam shook his head to clear his thoughts, as well as the mirage of Kate, and began his trudge through the frozen thicket, the underbrush flattened with snow, towards the beaver pond.

It wasn't long before the otter saw the snow-streaked edifices of the buildings that lined the pond's perimeter peeking through the scant tree line. It was said, at least according to Kate, that the old beavers once inhabited a great civilization, with the pond marking the center of their sprawling city. Sam was certain that they simply owned a

factory powered by the waterflow of their artificial pond, and
that they had abandoned their establishment, leaving it to the
mercy of the woods, once all the money dried up. Sam could
not say, however, that he didn't like Kate's version; the
enigmatic mysticism of it.

Sam wandered up to the edge of the pond, pushing through
the frozen reeds until he reached the first clean edges of ice.
The pond was frozen solid, a sheet of thick, foggy ice covering
its surface from bank to bank. Across the water, the derelict
ruins of the beaver factory loomed above the young otter, their
broken windows staring out like the black, alien eyes of some
long-forgotten god.

The scenery here was quiet, tranquil. A red-winged
blackbird darted out of the reeds and sailed through the air
across the pond. There was no wind, and the air smelled earthy
and fresh. Kate always spoke about how much she liked the
woods more than the water, but Sam could see why she liked it
here so much here despite the fact, why she'd go exploring
among the mud and ruins even though their parents warned
against it.

Sam picked up a tiny stone near his boot and tossed it
across the pond. He watched it skitter and slide, coming to rest
right in the center of the massive rink of ice. Somewhere, off in
the snowy boughs of the pines, an owl gave its ululating call.

Sam sighed heavily, slumping his shoulders, his tail and
whiskers drooping. The otter suddenly had no desire to go to
school.

"Come on," said the phantom Kate, her words materializing
in his ear. "Do it. Play hooky. You know you want to."

His brain said, don't do it, but his heart, ragged and torn
from all his longing and sadness, said stay away from school
today. Take a day off, rest your weary mind, and make sure to
spend your afternoon with someone who won't tell your
parents.

Mae was in the middle of baking fish crackers when Sam arrived, chilled and brooding, ashamed that he couldn't bear to go to school that day.

"Sam, hon, come in! Come in! It's too chilly for you to be out there all alone." The huge gator ushered Sam into her warm home, politely taking his coat and scarf to hang them up for him. "Say, shouldn't you be in school right now? It's Monday."

Sam froze in the middle of shucking off his boots, shame flashing across his face. "Yeah. It's just...I just couldn't –"

"It's alright." A clawed hand gently ruffled the fur between his ears. "We all have those days. I won't tell a soul."

Sam's throat felt like he'd swallowed a porcupine. He sniffled and wiped his nose with the back of a paw.

"I just feel like I'm having 'those' kind of days more often than not." He plunked down onto her plush, floral-patterned couch, watching the black and white TV in her living room flicker, its image distorted from the winter winds. "I just can't stop thinking about Kate and that dream."

"It's okay to think about her, Sam," said Mae as she came out of the kitchen, carrying a ceramic plate of warm fish crackers. She set it down on the coffee table in front of the couch.

"I know but..." Sam's whiskers trembled and a tear rolled down his cheek. He wiped it away, embarrassed. "It just hurts so much, I'm always thinking about her, always dreaming about her, even," he swallowed, "imagining that she's still here with me. Like a ghost." He stared at Mae through a shimmering mist of tears, as if the gator could somehow make it all better if he just begged her enough. "I miss her. I don't want her to be dead."

Mae sat down next to him and reached for his paw, taking it in hers and squeezing it. She waited for a long moment, letting the otter cry until he had no tears left to shed, before speaking.

"You know as well as I know that that girl be resting somewhere," the gator said softly.

Sam felt shocked, almost injured, by the gator's honesty; that she was bold enough to give voice to the truth that no one – not even Sam – wanted to face.

"Do you remember how Kate always said she wanted to be buried up on the hill that overlooks the beaver lake?" Mae continued. "She never wanted to be just another one of us water folk set off on a pyre. She wanted to rest among the trees."

Recovering from his shock, Sam bit his lip and nodded. "So you think she's 'resting' where she doesn't want to?"

Mae's amber eyes sparkled with some ageless wisdom that Sam could only hope to one day comprehend. "It's always a possibility."

"I don't really believe in ghosts." Sam shrugged his narrow shoulders. He reached for a cracker and bit into it. It was warm and sweet and salty, just how he liked them. "But, okay, even if I did, what can I do about it?"

"That's up for you to decide." Her massive, heavy tail thumped once against the side of the couch, and she gave him a wide, toothy grin. "You're her brother and you knew her best. She loved you, and still does."

Sam exhaled heavily and curled up on his side, stuffing one of the throw pillows beneath his head. "I don't know what to do. I just don't want to be sad anymore."

"Think it over and rest a while. It'll come to you." Mae grabbed the remote and switched the TV to a channel with cartoons before rising to her feet. "You can stay as long as you'd like, hon. I'll be in the kitchen tidying up. Gotta make sure everything is nice and pretty before I leave on Wednesday."

Sam abruptly sat up, his heart sinking. "You're leaving?"

"Alice's first clutch is just about ready to hatch." Alice was Mae's niece. Sam liked her from the few times he'd met her, but in that moment he hated her and all her unborn children. He didn't want Mae to leave. She couldn't leave him, not now! "I'm so excited for her, and I want to see the little lovelies as soon as they come crawling out of their shells."

"But you can't leave!" Sam suddenly found himself on his feet and before he knew it, he was clinging to her white and pink apron, burying his face into the scent of fabric softener and flour.

Mae knelt down and hugged him close. Sam rested his muzzle upon her wide, reptilian shoulders.

"It'll only be for a week, at the most," she said, petting the back of his head in an attempt to soothe. "Heaven knows I can't stand staying down in that place for long. Besides, you're a brave and smart boy. I'm sure you'll be fine without me for a bit."

"But I need you." He tightened his grip on her apron.

His mother was too depressed. His father was always working. His best friend – Kate herself – was dead. Mae was all he had left, his only real lifeline.

"I'll be back next Wednesday." She hugged him and he wished she would just pick him up and take him with her. "Stay strong, hon. I believe in you."

He was glad for her love, but he didn't know if he could stay strong. He didn't know if he could believe in himself.

Sam didn't dream again until the night Mae left.

The storm swirled around him, no longer playful flurries but a violent tempest racing through the trees, buffeting the otter as he trudged through a morass of snow that reached as high as his navel. He held up an arm to shield his face from the wind and pelting flakes, sharp as needles. Some distant part of him knew this was another dream, that he should just stop and try to wake himself up, but still he trudged forward into the whirling grey of the storm. Something called him, beckoned him, drew him in like a fish on a hook.

Then, through the veil she came, rising before him like a vengeful wraith. Her hair whipped wildly around her, black tendrils lashing about her shoulders and mask. Her robes billowed like blood red sails as she spread her arms. The lights appeared in their usual places, and she regarded Sam with her wordless stare.

The wind clawed at the otter, nearly knocking him to the ground. He suddenly felt angry. Tired of the dreams, of the games this spirit was playing with him.

He knew the woman wasn't Kate – there was no way. Kate wouldn't act like this towards him, all cryptic and secret. Kate had always been honest and blunt and straightforward. Who was this bizarre spirit, and why was it here?

The wind kicked up again, threatening to sweep Sam off his feet. He gritted his fangs and stepped forward, fighting against the gale force. Ice clung to his whiskers.

"Who are you?" It hurt to raise his voice above the wind's roar. "Why are you doing this to me?"

The phantom said nothing. Her ears seemed to change from those of a fox to those of a deer. Wind chimes sang among the wind's violent screams.

"Is this because of Kate?" Tears ran down his cheeks, turning to crystal beads that were quickly spirited away by the wind.

Ever silent, the phantom stared and around her the wisps of light grew brighter, brilliant flares in the obscuring curtain of snow.

But that didn't tell Sam anything. It only added to his frustration, his anger over how obtuse this nightmare was being. If it wanted to tell him something, or help him find his sister, why didn't it just say so?

The otter's body felt cold, but his heart swam with hot anger. He wanted Kate back, even if it was just to lay her to rest. He wanted closure, and his frustration – a bubbling froth of anger and sorrow – built in him like pressure in a bottle.

The winter hurricane swirled around him, roaring in his ears. Still, the wraith stared.

"Damn you!" The anger burst forth unexpectedly, a feeling as raw and harsh as the storm around him. Sam wrapped his arms around himself, feeling like his entire body were about to be ripped asunder. "What do you want from me?"

The world stopped, space and time suddenly frozen like ice. Neither the wind nor snow nor phantom moved. Even Sam himself stood frozen in time.

Then the world fell away, plunging them into a darkness so thick Sam could not see his own body, the only thing that remained were the three lights, blazing amidst the backdrop of purest night. Then, one by one, the lights winked out.

After that, Sam's dreams fell into a deep, dark nothingness.

It came to him in the darkness of that fitful slumber. If he couldn't bury Kate where she wanted to rest, he could at least bury something she loved. An item, a toy, something to draw her spirit away from where she didn't want to be and towards where she did. Sam didn't know if it would work, as if ghosts (if they even existed) could grow attached to certain items, but anything was worth an attempt. He knew Mae would be quite proud of him.

After coming home from school, he snuck upstairs to his sister's bedroom. His mother kept the room latched and untouched, a shrine to her dead, yet not-dead, daughter. No one was allowed in there, and Sam loitered in the hall for a good ten minutes, listening to his mother shuffling about downstairs in the kitchen as she prepared dinner, before ducking inside.

Everything was just as Kate had left it the night of her disappearance, untouched by time or living hands. Same old white dresser and matching bookcase (filled with more toys than books) with chipped paint. Same old bed, identical to Sam's, beneath the window, unmade and waiting for its occupant to return.

Sam could feel the familiar sadness returning. It looked like Kate might stroll in at any moment, even though he knew otherwise.

Sam refrained from touching anything, understanding deeply why his mother wanted to keep Kate's room a 'sacred place', though he found that made his search all the more difficult. He began looking around carefully, starting with the shelf, which was mainly stuffed animals and stacks of board games. None stood out to him as anything Kate cared deeply about. He moved to the bed and looked beneath it. Notebooks, a few more games. Nothing that felt overtly 'Kate'.

His hackles raised when he noticed the small cloth doll, her patchwork clothes red and her yarn hair as black as night. She was stitched out of an old white rag and had small, pointed ears, as well as a long tail. Sam recalled vague memories of him and Kate playfully arguing over whether the doll was a cat, a wolf, or a fox. Shivering, he turned away, afraid to touch that one trinket, no matter how appropriate it was for his task.

Fearing his mother, Sam paused briefly from his search and poked his head out into the hall. He exhaled with relief, detecting no sign of her, and when he ducked back inside, he saw the item that would be his trinket.

It was a small wooden fish, hand-carved and polished to a gleaming sheen. Its sides were decorated with swirling designs made of turquoise inlaid into the wood. Sam had bought it for Kate while on a school fieldtrip to an art museum. Kate had been ill, thus unable to attend, and while in the gift shop, Sam felt wrong buying something for himself and not for Kate. He hadn't thought the fish had been all that special, but Kate adored it and displayed it on her dresser ever since.

Sam took it, knowing it was perfect, and stowed it in the pocket of his coat. Then he went downstairs, again warily checking for his mother, before heading outside towards the wooded hill.

The snow was thinner beneath the pines, their thick canopy preventing it from piling high on the ground. Still, the frozen earth proved difficult, even for the otter's long claws, but through persistence and determination, he managed to dig a hole large enough for the figure. Sam set it down into its earthly tomb and, with ceremonial gentleness, smoothed the dirt over it until there was nothing left but a slightly raised mound of soil to mark its presence.

Sam stood, wiping his paws on his pants, feeling warm, yet not fulfilled. Something still felt hollow, but to symbolically bury Kate where she wanted was the best he could do.

Sam turned to leave the pine grove, and then, standing between two tall pines, was *her*.

She was just like in his dreams, a tall, ethereal thing of crimson robes and hair the color of night. Her mask was just as expressionless, just as ghostly pale. Her form shimmered between species – wolf, doe, rabbit – and Sam stood transfixed, unable to look away, the shock crashing down on him like a torrent of water. He blinked, expecting her to vanish, but she stayed, a silent, ghostly watcher.

Then, she turned tail and began to run.

"Wait!" Sam called after her, but she had already vanished over the crest of the hill.

Sam bolted after her and saw, through the thickening forest of trees, the phantom woman moving towards the beaver pond, a brilliant red blotch against the backdrop of white and grey

Sam followed her down the hill, stumbling over roots and branches hidden beneath the snow. At one point, he slipped and began to slide roughly down the slope on his rump, just barely regaining control over himself in time to narrowly avoid colliding with a tree. Sam could still see the woman, but she was far ahead and moving impossibly fast.

Panting, he got to his feet and continued running. "Wait up, please! I just want to talk!"

But the woman didn't wait. She kept gliding over the snow, eventually reaching the abandoned building on the shore and drifting inside.

Sam cursed and doubled his pace, out of breath and feeling ready to collapse once he reached the ramshackle building's flaky wooden door. His breath rushed out in heavy puffs of white, and his body ached for him to take a rest, but he couldn't stop now. He was so close to finding out the mystery of the red woman.

The door gave a shriek of protest as he pushed it in, its rusted hinges angry at having been woken up after so long.

"Hello?" Sam peered into the room, seeing nothing but hazy gloom. "Is anyone there?"

As his eyes adjusted, Sam saw more of what lurked inside. Most of the building had been gutted, but a few old hand tools gripped by fingers of rust sat forgotten on the sawdust-covered floor. A broken barrel shrouded in cobwebs rested at the base of the stairwell leading up to the second floor. Most of the windows were broken, and crystalline shards of glass glittered here and there near the walls. There seemed to be nothing out of the ordinary in the old building, until the otter glimpsed a flash of red ascending the stairs.

"Stop, please!"

His cry, however, went unanswered, so he dashed up the rickety stairway to the second landing. Above was much of the same, except one wall had partially fallen away, revealing what might have once been a balcony of sorts jutting over the water. Half the floor was covered in snow, and there was no sign of the wraith woman.

There was, however, a familiar pink strap peeking out from the mantle of white that covered the balcony.

Kate's bag! He'd know that strap anywhere.

Sam ran forward onto the balcony, his paw outstretched to grab the bag. Just as his claws closed around it, he heard a fibrous crack, and felt the floor shift beneath him. He looked down, and saw the derelict wooden balcony beginning to cave away beneath him, the wood far too aged and weathered to hold both otter and snow. He turned, but his short legs weren't fast enough; the balcony fell away with a thunderous, splintering crack, taking Sam with it.

He hit the ice hard enough to knock the wind out of him. All he could do for a moment was lay there and bask in the pain. His legs hurt, his back hurt, his lungs hurt. Sam's entire world was hurt and for a moment he almost thought he might black out form the pain of it all. However, soon the pain began to subside, and he found enough strength to sit up. He flexed his legs, then his arms, and finally his tail for good measure. Nothing seemed to be broken, just dreadfully sore.

When he stood, however, a new problem arose. With a sound that was almost electric in nature, a long series of cracks began to snake their away across the surface of the pond, starting just below the otter's boots. Eyes wide in fright, Sam took a cautious step back towards the shore, causing more cracks to dart out from beneath his boots. His heart hammered in his chest. Again, he took another step towards the shore.

The ice gave one last grating shriek before Sam fell through. Frigid water closed over him like a great hand as he sank into the pond's brackish, murky depths. Ordinarily, an otter like Sam could swim in icy ponds like this, but not while bogged down with heavy winter clothes that quickly became weighted and saturated by the chilly depths. He tried to kick his boots off, but he'd laced them so tight they refused to budge. Floundering, he tried to swim upward towards freedom, but his head bumped against a thick sheet of ice, trapping him like a pane of glass. In his struggles, he must have drifted in the darkness. His heart fluttered in his chest. Weeds coiled around his arms and legs, their touch filling him with dread. His fur protected him from the frigid temperature, but he hadn't had the time to take a proper breath before going under. His lungs began to burn, thirsting for a breath of oxygen. If he didn't escape quickly, Sam knew he would die.

Sam opened his eyes and fought against the icy needles that pierced his vision. Squinting against the agony, he looked upward and saw to his left the bright hole in the ice through which hazy sunlight shone through. He kicked towards it, but despite his conviction, Sam found his limbs didn't have the strength. Black specks began to encroach upon his vision, his lungs preparing to rebel at any moment. He began to sink into the murk and the waving, feathery arms of the weeds that reached up to receive him.

Even as the world began to darken, something small and gold caught his eye, glinting in the black muck. Mind going numb, Sam reached out with dream-like slowness to grasp it in a paw. His claws sank into the mud and silt, closing around the familiar trinket, which somehow felt warm against his furless palms.

It was Kate's ring, her favorite one, the one that never left her paw. She was here somewhere, he had found it, could sense it. Here in this pond. Here was where she died, where she was once lost, now found.

"Sam!" The voice rang out with crystal clarity despite the water that should have muffled it filling Sam's tiny ears. A voice as loving and familiar as the ring, though shrill now in its urgency. "Swim, Sam, swim!"

With the last of his strength, Sam forced his gaze to the shimmering surface. He could see her, just barely, through the crystal haze. Shadowed by a rippling figure of red stood Kate, one black paw reaching through the broken surface, questing towards her drowning brother. Lungs burning in agony, Sam kicked off the slippery bottom of the pond, propelling himself towards his sister's paw. He reached for her, his other hand still clutching her ring, and laced his fingers with hers. She felt warm, alive with love, though he knew in his shattered heart that she slept somewhere within those dark depths below.

He surfaced gasping for breath, his starving lungs practically singing with joy. In one last herculean effort, Sam clambered back onto the pond's icy surface and dragged himself up the reed-covered bank. His saturated clothing gave him the chills, and his eye were heavy with exhaustion, but he could hear the keening of sirens coming closer, and even as the weights of his eyelids fell, he knew he would be alright, that somehow he had been saved.

Sam was only saved because two other kids from his school happened to be digging around on the shore in search of cattail roots for dinner. He was lucky they'd seen him. If not, there would have been no ambulance, and had there been no ambulance, it was uncertain if he would have survived, even with the ghostly help he had received.

As Sam had learned that afternoon at the pond, Kate had indeed drowned. After Sam recovered from having nearly drowned himself, he showed his family the ring, which they too recognized as Kate's. He didn't mention the ghosts, or the dreams, or seeing her by the lake, but he knew he didn't have to. The day after he went home from the hospital, news came that her body had been found at the bottom of the beaver pond. She had fallen while playing in the old factory, hit her head on the rocks below, and subsequently drowned.

Her body was cremated privately, and though he wished she could have had a proper open-casket funeral, Sam was glad he hadn't seen it.

Per his request, they buried her up on the hill, in the woods she loved overlooking the pond. Sam cried and cried as they lowered the tiny box filled with the ashes that had been Kate into the ground, and when all was done, with Kate now sleeping where she always wanted to sleep, Sam dug up the figure he'd buried and set it on her grave alongside the white and red doll. The final goodbye from brother to sister.

He hadn't dreamed at all during his stay at the hospital, and now, finally back in his own bed, he went to sleep expecting to again relive that horrible nightmare. Instead, he found only peaceful darkness.

Mary E. Lowd

Mary E. Lowd writes stories and collects creatures. She's had more than 130 short stories published, and her novels include the Otters In Space trilogy, several spin-offs, and The Snake's Song: A Labyrinth of Souls Novel. Many of her novels feature cats who, deep down, wish they were otters. Her fiction has won an Ursa Major Award and two Cóyotl Awards. Meanwhile, she's collected a husband, daughter, son, bevy of cats and dogs, the occasional fish, and a multitude of imaginary otters. The stories, creatures, and Mary live together in a crashed spaceship disguised as a house, hidden inside a rose garden in Oregon. Learn more at **www.marylowd.com**.

THE BEST AND WORST
OF WORLDS

Five officers of the Tri-Galactic Navy and one exchange officer from the planet Cetazed teleported down to a clearing on Planet 328's surface. These cats and dogs were good people, and Consul Eliana Tor didn't regret leaving her homeworld to become an exchange officer. Not exactly. But she missed the flavor of the sunlight on Cetazed, and not only did her empathic abilities make her a fish out of water around these cats and dogs with their non-empathic minds, but they let her read the cats' and dogs' emotions—especially their feelings about her—constantly.

On her homeworld of Cetazed, Consul Tor had been surrounded by much stronger empaths and many telepaths. Among these Terran cats and dogs, however, her extremely poor empathic abilities became nearly a superpower. At first, their amusement at her coloring and shape—green like grass and lithe like a Terran otter—amused Eliana herself. She was happy to make them happy, even by playing the part of an exotic alien for them. But the novelty had worn off, and she worried that her people would be better off isolating themselves from these warm-blooded mammals.

Her people lived in peace on Cetazed: chlorophyllic otteroids in their cities of water parks. What need was there for gallivanting about the galaxy? Cats loved conquest; dogs needed adventure. But Cetazed otteroids were happy splashing about and playing.

Nonetheless, Consul Tor had to admit that this world they'd teleported down to was beautiful. The orange glow of a red dwarf, low on the horizon, mixed with the white-blue shine of another star at zenith made for a rich and complex flavor unlike anything Eliana had tasted on her homeworld. She rolled her shoulders, rippling her thick grass-like fur in order to savor the sunlight better. Unlike the navy officers, Eliana didn't wear a long-sleeved, long-legged uniform. She wore a strappy sundress, designed to expose as much of her fur to the light as possible while still maintaining warm-blooded definitions of decency.

"Enjoying the sunlight?" Commander Bill Wilker asked with a wolfish Collie grin. He was a handsome dog with flowing fur, and Consul Tor could read plainly in his feelings that he was taken with her.

"It's far better than the artificial lights onboard the Initiative," Consul Tor answered.

"Glad to hear it!" Cmdr. Wilker barked. Then he pulled out a unimeter, flipped open the hand-held device, and got right to work. He strode off toward the rest of his team, holding the unimeter in front of him and scanning the air and soil as he went.

Consul Tor pulled out her own unimeter to take readings on the sunlight from the different stars, but before she could finish her first scan, she felt a darkening. Consul Tor looked up at the sky, but it wasn't the stars—it was the emotions of the warm-blooded cats and dogs around her. They were scared.

"What happened?" Consul Tor asked. She approached Commander Wilker and the others; all five of the reconnaissance team members were staring into a canyon that cut steeply into the clearing. It didn't appear to be a natural formation. Rather it looked like an impact crater—a crash site for the broken, octagonal structure at its bottom. "A ship? Do you think there are any survivors?"

"I hope not," Cmdr. Wilker barked, his voice husky with the fear he was hiding from the two cats and two dogs under his command. He couldn't hide it from Consul Tor, and a sidelong glance at her with his worried brown eyes showed that he knew it. "We've encountered a ship like this one before."

One of the cats, an orange tabby wearing techno-focal goggles, piped up to add: "It did not go well."

One of the security officers, a yellow Labrador, simply started to growl.

"Hold on, guys," Cmdr. Wilker woofed, doing his best to sound soothing. "We don't know anything yet, so let's get some more information." He turned to the second cat, a science officer with glossy black fur and green eyes. "Lt. Unari, are there any life signs?"

Lt. Unari nearly purred the answer, "No, sir. No life signs. No survivors."

"That's a relief," the orange tabby meowed, and Consul Tor could feel how much he meant it. All of the reconnaissance team relaxed. Their relief hit Consul Tor like a wave, and it troubled her how pleased they were at the idea of the mysterious occupants of this crashed ship dying.

"Come on," Cmdr. Wilker barked. "The nature of our mission has changed: we need to get as much information as we can about this ship. Why's it here? What was it doing? Are there more of them? And we need to do it as fast as possible." He clambered over the edge of the cavern and slid his way down to the ship. The rest of the team followed, though Consul Tor could feel their reluctance. She didn't share it. The crashed ship was fascinating. She'd never seen architecture like it— layers of metal pipes and beams at sharp angles; lots of triangles and hexagons.

Cmdr. Wilker found a hatchway and burned it open with a beam of energy from his blazor. On the inside, ragged sheets of silvery silken fabric hung along the ceiling of the passageway, fluttering in the breeze from outside. Consul Tor could sense the rising terror in her companions—especially the orange tabby and yellow Labrador. She sensed very strongly that they'd been in a place like this before.

"We need to find the main computer," Lt. LeGuin, the orange tabby, said.

"Fan out," Cmdr. Wilker barked. "Scan everything. Get as much data as you can. This may be the best chance we get to learn about the Archidopterans before..." His voice broke, and he looked at Consul Tor, feeling a combination of trepidation and embarrassment that he couldn't hide his trepidation from her. "Never mind that. Just learn what you can and fast."

The cats and dogs disappeared down different passageways of the crashed spaceship, but Consul Tor simply stood in the entryway. She was shaken by the feelings she'd sensed in Cmdr. Wilker and needed to process them. He was deeply afraid. His mind had been filled with pictures of... violence and fighting... war. That's what this crashed spaceship represented to him: the potential for war coming to the Tri-Galactic Navy.

Consul Tor wrapped her short arms around herself, feeling suddenly cold without the sunlight against her green fur. Yet, she forged on, deeper into the dark ship, hoping to learn something that would help her reconcile Cmdr. Wilker's fears with the beautiful and intricate—delicate, even—architecture of this ship. The hanging silk whispered over her fur as she passed it by, touching her so lightly that it tasted almost like a flash of pale blue light.

She came to a chamber where the floor was covered with yellow orbs, each approximately the size of her own head. Consul Tor knelt down beside one of the orbs and peered closely at its yellow surface—it was filmy and slightly translucent. She could just make out angles and contours inside it, but not well enough to make sense of them. She pulled out her unimeter and scanned it; she was startled by the image that resolved on the unimeter screen: coiled and segmented, it was clearly the shape of a larval caterpillar-like insect. A baby that had died in its egg.

Now that she knew what she was looking at, Consul Tor could make out the wide round shape of its eyes underneath the filmy yellow surface of the egg. Her own feelings soured with sadness, and Consul Tor couldn't stay in that chamber for a moment longer. She hurried deeper into the ship.

The next chamber she came to was filled with mounds of the silver silk which she realized must be cocoons of some sort. Reluctantly, she scanned one of the cocoons and was rewarded with an image on her unimeter of an insectoid creature with all of its arms folded and its mandibled-head tucked against its chest. It looked peaceful in that pose, like it was sleeping, but she knew it would never wake up.

Consul Tor was deeply relieved when she heard barking, calling her back toward the entrance of the ship, away from this mausoleum.

"Time's up, everyone!" Cmdr. Wilker barked. "We have the computer's memory banks, and it's time to get out of here, on the double!" He gathered his team together, and then he tapped the comm-pin on the breast of his uniform and told the TGN Initiative to teleport them back up to the ship in orbit.

Captain Pierre Jacques kept exquisite control of his emotions as the reconnaissance team briefed him on the information they'd gathered aboard the Archidopteran ship. He was a Sphynx cat with incredible composure; his naked pink triangular ears didn't flick even once as Lt. LeGuin, the orange tabby engineer with techno-focal goggles, showed him the data from the crashed ship's computer banks. Only Consul Tor could tell that Captain Jacques was scared.

And he was scared.

"These are battle plans," the captain meowed, cool as a cat could be. But on the inside he was raging with turmoil.

Cmdr. Wilker, however, was much calmer than he'd been

on the planet. Consul Tor had noticed that he was always calmer when the captain was around. Although the Sphynx cat was only half the collie's height, Captain Jacques' mere presence seemed to soothe Cmdr. Wilker.

"Yes, sir," Cmdr. Wilker agreed. "But we caught their plans early. I think we can cut off their fleet before it's able to do any real damage to any TGN star bases."

Captain Jacques' gray-green eyes narrowed. "Unless it's a trap." He hissed the words.

"Captain, if I may say something—" Consul Tor's voice was high and piping next to the barks and meows of the others. "—the chambers on the vessel that I examined were filled with unhatched eggs and cocoons. Many of these aliens' young died on that ship. So, if it's a trap for us, it's one that came to them at a high cost."

The emotions of the cats and dogs around Consul Tor churned with a mix of disgust at the very idea of Archidopteran reproduction and disbelief that such a species even cared about their offspring.

With dawning horror, Consul Tor felt the depth of the gulf between her and these mammals. Their empathy was so shallow, extended only to creatures they found esthetically pleasing

"Shame on all of you," Consul Tor intoned. "Do you doubt that my people care for their offspring simply because we reproduce by budding flowers?" She stared down each of the cats and dogs in the room before adding, "Clearly, this has entered the realm of official Tri-Galactic Navy business. I'll be in my quarters if my counsel is needed."

Consul Tor's quarters on the TGN Initiative had been retrofitted with a large sauna bath where she could soak in mineral water and absorb the nutrients she didn't get from sunlight. It was a meditative place, not at all like the pools on her homeworld where she was used to frolicking and splashing.

So, when the door to her quarters chimed, indicating a visitor, Consul Tor was deep in thought. She dripped her way to the door, told it to open, and found Captain Jacques standing on the other side. His naked pink ears were splayed, and his feelings were divided, distracted, and tumultuous. "May I come in?" the Sphynx cat asked.

Consul Tor stepped aside and said, "By all means. Do you mind if I swim while we talk?"

"Not at all," the captain answered, clearly amused. He didn't seem to have the instinctive distaste for water that most cats on the ship did. With his hairless skin, he didn't have fur to get wet.

The captain settled on a cushioned ledge under the room's wide star-studded window, and Consul Tor slipped back into the mineral water, feeling it work its way into her fur, fluffing and nourishing it.

"You have a different perspective than anyone else on my crew," the captain meowed. "I value that, and I want to understand it."

While swimming lazy laps on her back around the small pool, Consol Tor said, "I see beauty in those aliens."

"I see danger," the captain countered.

"Your vision is clouded by fear. That makes you think that you see danger."

The captain considered her words very carefully. The tip of his naked tail twitched as if setting out a rhythm for his thoughts. "That's possible," he admitted. "We met the Archidopterans before under very different—and troubling—circumstances."

Consul Tor savored the change she sensed in the captain's emotions as the pink-skinned cat allowed himself to be soothed by her perspective.

"I will think on this," Captain Jacques said. "And I'll keep it under advisement when we face the Archidopterans."

"When we face them?" Consul Tor asked.

"A fleet of their ships are approaching Old Earth—the seat of the Tri-Galactic Navy and my own homeworld. It would be a devastating military target, and we plan to cut them off before they get there." His tail twitched and the unease in his feelings returned, yet weaker than it had been before. "I hope that you are right, and it can be a peaceful encounter."

The captain got up to leave, but he turned back before going through the door, tail swishing jauntily. "I'd like you to be on the bridge for the encounter. I think your presence might be invaluable."

The captain had doubts, but he chose to embrace hope. For now, the symbol of hope in his mind was a green otter. Consul Tor could live with that.

The fleet of Archidopteran vessels were arranged in a v-like formation, like geese flying home, but they weren't flying to their own home. They were flying towards the home of most of the cats and dogs on the TGN Initiative. Consul Tor felt the fear of the navy officers as they watched the angular icosahedral vessels grow larger on the Initiative's viewscreen.

"Open a communication channel to the lead vessel," Captain Jacques ordered.

A terrier at the helm said, "Channel open."

Captain Jacques straightened the jacket of his navy uniform and spoke to the main viewscreen, "This is Captain Pierre Jacques of the Tri-Galactic Navy ship Initiative. I wish to offer you a peaceful welcome to this sector of space."

The other cats and dogs on the bridge stared at their captain with quizzical, confused expressions. The yellow lab, Security Chief Natalie Vonn, was trying to figure out if the small Sphynx cat had gone completely crazy. But none of them dared question the captain. They trusted him too much.

"No response," the terrier at the helm said.

The captain harrumphed and swished his naked tail. "Let's try again, shall we?"

"I guess?" the terrier said, looking extremely confused. The captain glared at him until he added, "Channel open."

"I'd like to invite a delegation of your officers aboard our ship—"

From the back of the bridge, Lt. Vonn couldn't suppress a whimper-whine at the idea of willingly inviting Archidopterans onto the Initiative.

"—for a tour, refreshments, and open discussion of your fleet's plans in this sector of space." The captain's whiskers rose in a smile, and Consul Tor could sense he was immensely pleased with himself for doing the right thing and offering hospitality to this alien race. She was pleased with him as well.

Then he disappeared in a sparkly shimmer of quantum energy. Shock spread through all of the officers on the bridge

"What the hell!" Cmdr. Wilker barked. The collie rushed to the empty space where the captain had been, twirled around several times as if looking for him, and then turned to growl at the viewscreen. "Open a channel," he snapped, but before the terrier at the helm could follow his order, a message from the Archidopteran vessel appeared on the viewscreen.

The image of the icosahedral vessels disappeared, replaced by an image of an Archidopteran itself: its silver carapace gleamed, and its many-jointed arms moved restlessly; shimmery wings flapped slowly behind it; the antennae on its head and glittering compound eyes stared relentlessly at the screen; when its wriggling mouth parts and pincer-like mandibles began to move, it emitted a sound like a chainsaw squealing against metal. All of the cats on the bridge flattened their ears, and the dogs rolled their heads, trying to escape the horrible sound.

But Consul Tor heard the meaning inside it—not through words, but through feelings. The green otteroid spoke, translating what she understood as it came to her: "The Archidopteran Queen needs new worlds for her eggs and new worker drones to tend them. Our ship is too small for her to bother with us, but she's taken our captain as a warning: don't interfere." Consul Tor felt a mix of responsibility for what had happened and frustration with these aliens' seeming inability to communicate with each other

Anger flared inside Cmdr. Wilker like a bonfire. Underneath his flowing fur, he filled with razor-sharp hate so strong that it buffeted Consul Tor's mind with actual words: my sheep, my ward, my alpha. Consul Tor didn't know what those words meant, but they clearly meant a lot to him.

Cmdr. Wilker woofed, "We must rescue the captain." He spoke the words as simple, empirical truth, but then he looked around the bridge and saw the other navy officers watching him, waiting for their orders. Without the captain, he was in charge. These were his wards, his sheep—he was their sheepdog, their alpha. He couldn't chase the captain, not until the rest of his flock was safe. Sadness doused the fire inside him, and he grew cold. "But first, lay in a course for the nearest Tri-Galactic Navy star base. We need to regroup. We need reinforcements."

Consul Tor watched the Tri-Galactic Navy vessels take formation through the window in her quarters. They were very different from the geometrical Archidopteran ships—all smooth edges and curves. Very graceful. These ships had a streamlined quality, almost like toys that an otteroid budling might build, gluing together river-bottom pebbles and bits of stick.

But these toy ships held hundreds of lives each. And they were preparing for battle. Even if they won, how many Archidopteran lives would it cost?

Consul Tor knew that Cmdr. Wilker was meeting with the captains of the other vessels in the Initiative's conference room right that minute, planning how their fleet would surround the Archidopterans, cut them off from Earth, demand they reverse course, and destroy them if they didn't. It was violent. And Consul Tor hated it.

If Captain Jacques were still here, she might have been included in the meeting, and perhaps she could have tempered their plan. Softened it. Though that hadn't worked well before... She still wasn't ready to give up on peace with the Archidopterans.

However, Captain Jacques was not here, and Cmdr. Wilker's feelings made it perfectly clear that the collie blamed Consul Tor for that. He blamed her, and he wanted her to stay away from him.

So, she watched the pebble-and-stick ships arrange themselves in a grid in front of the stars, and she came up with a plan.

If she couldn't convince Cmdr. Wilker to seek peace with the Archidopterans himself, maybe she could seek it for him. She simply had to offer her services to him in a way he could understand: she would volunteer to teleport aboard the Archidopteran flagship during the battle and attempt to rescue the captain. He wouldn't be able to resist that. And once she was over there, maybe she could find a way to broker peace with the Archidopterans.

Cmdr. Wilker accepted Consul Tor's plan with a few modifications. Instead of teleporting to the Archidopteran ship, she had to take a shuttle. And she couldn't go alone. He insisted on her taking Lt. Vonn, the yellow lab security officer, and Lt. LeGuin, the orange tabby engineer, with her. Apparently, they had the most experience dealing with Archidopteran vessels, as they'd been on the reconnaissance team when the Initiative had first encountered one.

Of course, this also meant they had the most baggage and

hostile feelings concerning the Archidopterans. Consul Tor saw that as a distinct disadvantage, but Cmdr. Wilker didn't. And he was in charge.

Consul Tor's shuttle launched from the Initiative during the heat of battle. Lt. LeGuin skillfully piloted the small vessel, dodging both enemy and friendly fire, while the Initiative laid down a volley of electron torpedoes as cover. It was their hope that in all the chaos, the Archidopterans wouldn't notice such a small, relatively insignificant shuttle craft. Or else, they wouldn't have the resources available to target it.

As a red bolt of energy singed past the shuttle's viewscreen, Consul Tor swore and exclaimed, "What in the hell was that collie dog thinking, sending us in a shuttle when we could have teleported!"

Lt. Vonn was eerily calm as she answered from the back of the shuttle, "He was thinking that last time we were on one of these vessels, they had technology that could block our comm-pins and possibly our teleporters." The yellow lab wasn't paying any attention to the space battle happening all around them. She was busy checking her sidearms. She had various blazors and vibro-knives strapped to every one of her limbs. Consul Tor wouldn't have been surprised to find a weapon hidden in the swishing brush of her tail. "He doesn't want us to get stuck over there."

Consul Tor didn't understand the existential horror that emanated from the orange tabby piloting their shuttle at the words 'stuck over there.' As far as she could tell, these dogs and cats had started this war, and while they looked superficially more similar to her than the Archidopterans, her underlying anatomical structure—beneath the grassy green fur—was more similar to the sessile plants they kept as decorations. She was beginning to wonder why her species had felt any kinship with the members of the Tri-Galactic Navy when they'd come to her homeworld.

After several more red bolts of energy singed by, close enough to warm the air inside the shuttle, Lt. LeGuin exclaimed, "Hold on, here comes the big one!" Sure enough, moments later, sparks and fire engulfed the side of the Archidopteran vessel as an electron torpedo from the <u>Initiative</u> tore a hole in its side, calculated to blow open a portion of the ship's shuttle bay. Atmosphere exploded outward and then fizzled in the vacuum of space.

Under cover of the explosion, Lt. LeGuin piloted their shuttle into the newly gaping open enemy shuttle bay. Exactly as planned. Moments later, a shimmery force field sealed off the gaping hole in the shuttle bay's doors, but the <u>Initiative</u> reconnaissance team was already safely inside.

Lt. Vonn held out a blazor rifle to Consul Tor as they debarked the shuttle. "Take this," the yellow lab said, but the green otteroid stared at the rifle like it was a squirming snake... or whatever photosynthetic aliens find disgusting. Lt. Vonn could not understand this exchange officer. "You need to protect yourself," she barked.

"I thought that's what you're here for." Consul Tor still didn't take the rifle, but she stepped out onto the deck of the Archidopteran vessel, edging around the large yellow lab.

Lt. Vonn growled deep in her throat, and the short blonde fur around her neck prickled out. "Suit yourself." She handed the rifle to Lt. LeGuin, and the orange tabby took it without hesitation. "You stay here and guard the shuttle," Lt. Vonn barked at him. "The Consul and I will get back here with the captain as fast as possible, and I expect we'll need to make a quick exit."

"Getaway detail," Lt. LeGuin meowed. "Got it. And I can't say I mind. I don't envy you guys, heading out there." Streams of text flowed over the lenses of the little cat's techno-focal goggles. "Good luck."

"All right, Consul," Lt. Vonn barked, "you're leading this

detail, so where to?"

Consul Tor unholstered the unimeter at her waist and stared at the data and scans on the device's screen. Based on electro, magnetic, heat, and sonar scans, it projected a map of their surroundings and pinpointed the locations of nearby life signs. It also showed the location of the captain's comm-pin—in a large chamber, mostly empty of life signs, down several passageways to the right—but Consul Tor didn't feel right about that.

The empathic green otteroid felt drawn to a smaller chamber, packed full of life signs, further away to the left. If she explained herself to the security dog, Consul Tor knew Lt. Vonn would insist they head toward the comm-pin.

Consul Tor made her decision. "This way." She darted through the severely damaged shuttle bay, trying hard not to look at the shimmery force field protecting them from the gaping hole the Initiative had blown to get them in.

Through the force field's shimmery light, Consul Tor could see the Tri-Galactic Navy vessels and the Archidopteran ships firing at each other. Destroying each other. So much death. She had to shut it out—she had to focus on the whisper she heard calling to her from inside this vessel. She led Lt. Vonn down the chamber to the left.

Consul Tor glanced occasionally at the unimeter clutched in her paws, keeping an eye on the various life signs—especially those moving through the corridors. Though, she found that she could sense the presence of the moving life signs as clearly in her mind—a bold, brazen, uncompromising sensation—as on the unimeter's screen. When one of those life signs came too close, Consul Tor took a risk and ducked into a small chamber—according to the unimeter, it was a chamber filled with life signs, but in her own mind... All she could hear were quiet murmurs. Daydreams. Or perhaps, lullabies.

Sure enough, inside the chamber, Consul Tor found a trove

of the waist-high, golden eggs like she'd found on the crashed vessel that had started all of this. She crouched down behind one of them, and Lt. Vonn followed suit. The yellow Labrador looked funny with her tongue hanging out, panting, as she tried to fit behind one of the yellow orbs. Though, Consul Tor could sense that her emotions were anything but funny—Lt. Vonn was more than ready to use the blazor rifle grasped in her paws.

"Wait," Consul Tor said, holding out a green-furred paw in a steadying gesture. "If we can stay hidden and do as little damage as possible..." How could she explain this to such a battle-ready warmongering dog?

"I get it," Lt. Vonn woofed quietly. "Low profile. Any idea how close we are..." The yellow lab's voice trailed off as an Archidopteran skittered its way down the hall outside the chamber.

Consul Tor only got a brief glimpse of the hulking metallic body, but she thought the Archidopteran's translucent wings and shining carapace were beautiful. The silvery surface of its body made her think of stream reflecting the sky, and its wings looked like lace. Lt. Vonn, on the other paw, was about to go out of her mind with fear. Consul Tor didn't love that she was accompanied by a well-armed emotional wreck. She'd have much preferred completing this mission alone.

Before leaving the egg chamber, Consul Tor pressed one of her green paws up against one of the golden eggs. She felt a babbling voice of confusion and surprise and delight from inside. Then she heard the disjointed, sing-song tones of a babbling baby trying to repeat a lullaby.

"Ugh," Lt. Vonn woofed, looking at the squirming caterpillar-like shape under the translucent surface of the egg. "These things are hideous. Can we move on?"

Regretfully, Consul Tor pulled her paw away from the egg and led them on. She would have liked to stay and hear more of the lullaby, but without her paw pressed against the egg's warm surface, all she heard were distant whispers, disappearing as she forged deeper into the Archidopteran vessel.

Yet, another whisper called her onward. It grew stronger with every step, until she could almost hear an actual voice echoing in her head. She couldn't make out words, but she felt the shapes of words. She recognized the voice as the captain's... but then it was someone else. It morphed, dizzyingly, until a single phrase rang out like a bell: "Conflict is fruitless."

Consul Tor stumbled, and Lt. Vonn caught her. "Are you okay?" the yellow lab asked.

The voice in Consul Tor's mind had been seductive and powerful, and it spoke words she agreed with: times of conflict never coincided with a time of fruiting for her people. "Did you hear that?" she asked Lt. Vonn.

The yellow lab shook her head, muzzle drawn into a serious grimace.

The voice spoke in Consul Tor's mind again: "The mammals can't hear me without... help. I am the voice of the many. The All-Mother. The Queen. Yet, you are not my child, and you can hear me, little flower." One voice and yet thousands. And the captain's voice was woven into the tapestry with the rest.

"Maybe we should go back," Lt. Vonn woofed nervously. "I'm not sure I can carry both you and the captain safely, if we find him."

"I'm fine," Consul Tor snapped, pushing the yellow lab away from her. "We're close now." She was sure of it. But she wasn't sure it mattered anymore.

Consul Tor continued onward, and the voice continued singing in her head: "That's right, little flower. Bring the mammal to me, and I'll help her understand."

The physical world became illusory under Consul Tor's green paws. With each step down the passageway, her senses filled with a warm glow like the light of a red-orange sun. She could picture every ticking machination of the hive around her—workers with their tiny vestigial wings and strong six-arms tending to the ship; drones with their hulking height, true wings, and delicate six-arms, tending the eggs and cocoons. The eggs and cocoons themselves, singing in their slumber, praising the harmony of the hive, the placid wisdom of the Queen, their protector.

The Queen herself, enthroned in the heart of the vessel, almost the very vessel itself, seeing through its sensors, fighting the Tri-Galactic Navy vessels with her weaponry.

Consul Tor swooned, and Lt. Vonn caught her up. "I'm taking you back to the shuttle," the yellow lab barked, too scared to modulate her voice to a quiet woof.

"No," Consul Tor said, but it wasn't her voice anymore. She was one of the queen's children. Adopted and strange, but loved. She held out a green-furred paw and pointed into the next chamber. "Right there. What you're seeking is right in there."

"You're being so weird," Lt. Vonn woofed, finding her control again. It gave her something to focus on—protecting the green otteroid draped over her yellow-furred arms. In that way, Lt. Vonn was like the Queen—a protector—but so much smaller.

Lt. Vonn carried Consul Tor into the chamber. By then, the green otteroid was completely lost in visions of the queen's harmony. Overwhelmed by the voices of the hive. Of course, all Lt. Vonn knew was that the delicate photosynthetic alien had fainted in her arms, and the yellow lab would have to carry both the otteroid and the captain back to the shuttle if he'd been incapacitated—meaning her arms would be full. She'd be a sitting duck, unable to properly defend herself or her wards.

Lt. Vonn needed to get the reconnaissance team out of here.

Unfortunately, the captain wasn't obviously inside the

chamber the Consul had indicated. All Lt. Vonn saw inside were a bunch of silken mounds. With horror, she realized she'd seen mounds like this before—the last time the <u>Initiative</u> had encountered the Archidopterans. They were cocoons.

Lt. Vonn laid the Consul down on the floor and began ripping into the nearest cocoon with her bare paws, scrabbling at the sticky silk with her dull claws. It would have been faster to cut her way through the silk with a vibro-knife, but what if the captain was inside? What if she cut too deep?

The silk tore away, and under the tear, Lt. Vonn revealed segmented arms, folded as if in prayer, and a gun-metal gray carapace. Not the captain. Oh god, she hoped it was not the captain. He couldn't have been transformed so fully?

Lt. Vonn began ripping away at another cocoon and found another pupal Archidopteran beneath the silk. Another and another. She left the cocoons shredded, and the pupae underneath began stirring, their many segmented legs twitching and antennae feeling around to taste the air in their new, adult forms. Another few minutes, and they'd be fully awake.

They'd be ready to wrap Lt. Vonn inside her own cocoon.

But then Lt. Vonn ripped through the silk of a smallish cocoon and found something different: segmented legs, folded as if in prayer... but they were pink. Like the captain's naked skin. With a sinking feeling, Lt. Vonn ripped more of the silk off and revealed a hideous hybrid, half Sphynx cat and half Archidopteran. The captain had grown antennae beside his triangular ears, and his muzzle had morphed into wide mandibles filled with writhing mouth parts.

But his gray-green eyes were the same.

Except filled with horror.

"Oh Captain," Lt. Vonn breathed. Her heart ached for the little cat, and her stomach churned with revulsion. She pulled the rest of the silk away from him and threw his small, strange body over one shoulder.

Then Lt. Vonn lifted the Consul from the floor and draped the otteroid's limp body over the other shoulder. The Consul's thick green fur had become studded with tiny star-like white flowers. Lt. Vonn didn't know what that meant, but the yellow lab knew that she needed to get out of here. Now.

But of course, the entrance to the chamber was blocked by a pair of Archidopterans, and the pupae that Lt. Vonn had freed early from their cocoons rose from their positions of repose, unfolding their arms and clacking their mandibles. The room was filled with towering insectoids, and Lt. Vonn didn't have half a chance of shooting her way out.

So, instead, she whispered a prayer and tapped the comm-pin on her breast. "Lt. LeGuin?" she barked. "Please for the sake of everything holy, tell me that you're receiving this and that the shuttle's teleporter isn't blocked by this ungodly ship's shields."

The Archidopterans encircled Lt. Vonn, raising their upper-most arms like they were dancing. One after another, the towering insectoids spat globs of sticky silk against the growling yellow Labrador.

Even through the deafening harmonies of the hive filling her mind, Consul Tor felt her fellow officer's terror—a discordant note that pierced through her, wringing her with complex tendrils of regret. She had led the yellow dog here. She had trusted in the Archidopterans' good faith and her own ability to bring everyone into accordance. But the only accord the Archidopterans offered was annihilation. And violation. She had never imagined before that her own empathy could be used against her, but the voice of the hive buzzed inside of her, pushing at her, leaving no space for herself.

Then the orange tabby's voice meowed from Lt. Vonn's comm-pin, "I can probably get off one teleportation before they block us, but I need an active comm-pin signal to lock onto."

"Not a problem; the captain and Consul Tor are in my arms!" On the final word, a glob of sticky silk hit Lt. Vonn in the face, filling her open mouth with a musty taste that made her gag and glued her muzzle shut. But then she felt the tingle of quantum energy in her chest, and her body flooded with relief.

The yellow lab, transmuted Sphynx cat, and photosynthetic otteroid disappeared in a shimmer of quantum energy and reappeared inside their own shuttle, where they promptly fell over, crashing onto the ground, too glued together by silk to do anything but lay there uselessly while Lt. LeGuin meowed at them.

"My goodness, but you three look a horror. I'm getting us out of here." The orange tabby kept them updated with a running monologue as he powered up the shuttle, fired an electron torpedo at the force field holding them in, and then piloted the shuttle back out of the Archidopteran vessel.

As the shuttle dodged electron torpedoes and red energy bolts, flying back through the fray towards the Initiative, something strange was happening on the deck inside. Lt. Vonn was struck by the beautiful harmony of the Archidopteran hive; Consul Tor felt her mind fill with terror at losing herself—was she even a cat anymore? Wait, had she ever been one? And Captain Jacques was flooded by the sense of safety and assurance that came with being the greatest breed of dog ever designed by man—a yellow Labrador was protected from all harm by the great love that had gone into designing it. His paws were big. Her ears floppy. He was a good... hive member who loved her Queen?

Lt. LeGuin piloted the shuttle back into the relative safety of the Initiative's own welcoming shuttle bay. On the shuttle's floor, the rest of the reconnaissance team blurred and melded together, aided by Consul Tor's empathic abilities and the catalytic enzymes in the silk that half cocooned them together.

Instead of a dog, a cat, and an otteroid, they'd become a mess of segmented legs, green and yellow fur, pink skin, and three pairs of eyes filled with deep, existential horror. They could see themself in the reflection of Lt. LeGuin's techno-focal goggles, as the orange tabby hit the comm-pin on his breast and meowed, "Doctor Keller, we have an emergency in the shuttle bay."

Consul Tor felt the captain's concern for his crew and Lt. Vonn's frustration with herself that she was lying on a bed in the medical bay rather than doing her job.

But... they were just feelings. Sensations that she could sense from outside of herself. No longer her own thoughts.

Consul Tor lifted her green-furred paws and held them above her face. They looked normal. The embarrassing white flowers were gone. She shouldn't have been flowering at all. Not now. Not like that. She lifted herself up and looked around.

Lt. Vonn was lazing on her hospital bed, bouncing a ball off of the nearest wall to pass the time. Captain Jacques was a normal Sphynx cat again, and he held a dusty old book in his paws. But Consul Tor could tell he wasn't able to concentrate on reading it.

"You're awake!" a cheerful voice barked. Doctor Keller was a tall red dog with long curly ears. An Irish Setter and proud of it. A lot of the dogs onboard this vessel seemed inordinately proud of themselves, simply for being a particular type of dog.

Consul Tor shook her head at the strangeness of it. And yet, she'd experienced the sensation first-hand while she'd been melded with the captain and Lt. Vonn. It was a strange but harmless kind of pride.

While the doctor checked Consul Tor, scanning her with a unimeter and muttering about her alien physiology, another prideful dog burst into the medical bay.

But Cmdr. Bill Wilker wasn't proud of himself for being a dog right now. He was bursting with pride on behalf of... Consul Tor. The green otteroid felt a bashful modesty at the bright glow of Cmdr. Wilker's pride in her.

"Our hero has awoken!" he barked, rushing to Consul Tor's side. He took one of her green paws in his own and squeezed tight. "Thank you," the collie woofed. "You saved the captain."

"Lt. Vonn and Lt. LeGuin saved the captain, I think," Consul Tor said, lowering her eyes from the collie's intense gaze.

Lt. Vonn paused in bouncing her ball and gave the Consul a curt, appreciative nod. Then back to bouncing.

"They wouldn't have been over there without you." Cmdr. Wilker smoothed the flowing fur of his ruff that spilled out around his collar. "Besides, I've thanked each of them already. Lt. LeGuin as soon as he got back, and Lt. Vonn when she woke up a week ago."

"A week ago?" Consul Tor asked. "Has it been so long? What happened to the rest of the ship? All the other ships? Are we still fighting?"

Captain Jacques laid his dusty book down on his lap. "We won the battle. The jury's still out on the war." His pink ears flattened. "And yes, we've been trapped in this godforsaken sick bay all week."

"The flagship exploded only minutes after your shuttle escaped," Cmdr. Wilker barked. "After the flagship was destroyed, all the other ships... They ran out of fight. They simply withdrew from the sector, back the way they came."

"Good riddance," Lt. Vonn muttered, throwing her ball extra hard.

Consul Tor felt a confusing wave of loss. The Archidopteran Queen had manipulated her mind, altered the captain's body against his will, and would have experimented with her reproductive flowers if Lt. Vonn hadn't rescued her.

Yet, the harmony of her hive had been beautiful. All those voices, joined together as one, in perfect accord and completely loved.

It wasn't worth it. The price for that accord and harmony was high. Much too high.

In comparison, the dogs and cats of the Tri-Galactic Navy were noisy and disjointed, a constant jumble of conflict and mixed-up emotions. They were chaotic. Uncontrollable. And they had saved the entire sector from the Archidopterans.

And Consul Tor loved them.

About the Editor

A small-clawed otter born in Waukesha Wisconsin in 1994, SignificantOtter, also known as John Kulp, has steadily moved Southeast his entire life. After attending the University of Pittsburgh for a double degree in Computer Science and Japanese, he relocated to Philadelphia to work at a start-up as a full stack web developer.

John currently resides by the Schuylkill River, where he's evaded several attempts by the coast guard to remove him. He enjoys playing board games, running along the shore, and imbibing impossible quantities of tea. His weekends are spent writing, hiking, and tabletop role-playing. You can follow him on Twitter at @RunningOtter.

About the Artist

Jasmin "Kippy" Gröhn is a digital artist in her late 20s currently residing in a small town in southern Finland with her pet rabbit. She specializes in realistic animal drawings and paintings, and sometimes likes to add a twist of fantasy in them. She has drawn since childhood, but started drawing more seriously in her teenage years. She is a completely self-taught artist. You can find her work online on Twitter at https://twitter.com/kippycube and on Artstation at https://jgrohn.artstation.com.